SECRETS BENEATH A RIVIERA SKY

JENNIFER BOHNET

Boldwood

First published in Great Britain in 2025 by Boldwood Books Ltd.

Copyright © Jennifer Bohnet, 2025

Cover Design by Debbie Clement Design

Cover Images: Shutterstock

A CIP catalogue record for this book is available from the British Library.

Paperback ISBN 978-1-80162-314-8

Large Print ISBN 978-1-80162-313-1

Hardback ISBN 978-1-80162-312-4

Ebook ISBN 978-1-80162-316-2

Kindle ISBN 978-1-80162-315-5

Audio CD ISBN 978-1-80162-307-0

MP3 CD ISBN 978-1-80162-308-7

Digital audio download ISBN 978-1-80162-310-0

This book is printed on certified sustainable paper. Boldwood Books is dedicated to putting sustainability at the heart of our business. For more information please visit https://www.boldwoodbooks.com/about-us/sustainability/

Boldwood Books Ltd, 23 Bowerdean Street, London, SW6 3TN

www.boldwoodbooks.com

'You can't go back, but you can move forward'

— ERNEST HEMINGWAY

1

Agnes stared out at the rain-soaked garden as Theo's voice, suitably sombre, but without an apologetic, 'I'm sorry for the sad call', informed her of the death of his brother, her husband. The phrase 'Oscar is dead' hung in the silence of the airwaves for several seconds and failed to elicit the correct emotion in her.

'Had he been ill?' She pulled herself together enough to ask.

'*Non*. He fell off his boat and drowned.'

Theo's matter of fact voice lacked any sorrow or regret in its measured tones. Perhaps it was the telephone line masking his emotions? It was his older brother after all, even if they were constantly falling out. Agnes knew though that she and Theo were emotionally as one on the subject of Oscar Agistini. Thankfully, and seemingly knowing without asking, that she wouldn't be rushing over to France, Theo told her he would deal with the funeral arrangements and call again with the details.

'Would you like me to phone Francine and tell her?' Theo asked finally.

'*Non merci*. I will tell her.' She knew her daughter would have a similar reaction as her own to the news. When the call ended,

Agnes found it impossible to remember it in detail. In truth it had been a strange, one-sided conversation. She, unable to express an unfelt sorrow, Theo simply doing his duty informing her of the facts. Conversation about the event would follow later without a doubt.

How was she supposed to feel about the death of a man she hadn't seen for far too many years to count, Agnes wondered? The truth was she didn't feel a thing – no sadness for his death, no regret for the way things were, no guilt for her part in... anything. She might still bear his surname but Oscar had ceased to have a meaningful existence in her life over forty years ago. She'd routinely wished him dead and buried for so long that the unexpected, if welcome, news of his demise was hard to take in.

Had there been any truth in the power of murderous thoughts, the ones she'd harboured and sent his way down through the years should have been enough to kill him off a long time ago. As should the straw doll she'd kept hidden in the dressing table drawer and stuck pins into on and off for years. Relieving her frustration over her situation by repeatedly jabbing an old hat pin into the stuffed doll and slamming it hard against the wall had been so therapeutic. Until it came to an abrupt end a decade ago. After a particularly upsetting row with Oscar, she'd managed to stab her own finger rather than the doll and got blood all over it. Soaking the doll in warm water in an effort to clean it proved to be a bad idea as it disintegrated so she'd thrown the remains in the rubbish bin.

Age had thankfully worn away her frustration with certain life events and she rarely felt the need to vent her feelings these days by sticking pins in dolls. If she did, she merely stamped her feet like a petulant toddler for thirty seconds or so before pouring herself a small sherry and letting the feeling go. Sherry. She could do with one right now. Taking the bottle of her favourite dry sherry out of the fridge Agnes poured herself a glass and took a sip.

The day she'd left France all those years ago she'd vowed never to return to the Riviera while Oscar was still alive. Now he was dead and she could return. Thoughtfully she sipped her drink. But was it all too late? If only he'd died thirty, forty, years ago there would have been a point in returning, time would have been on her side. But now? Agnes gave a mental shrug.

The world had moved on, she was officially an old woman and even if she did return it would all be so, so different. Life here in Dartmouth, South Devon had settled onto an even keel over the years and was good. Going back would surely drag the past into the present, bringing a bundle of regrets with it that would weigh her down rather than uplift her.

The foolish thing though, was that she wasn't sure she could deny herself one last opportunity to try and make peace with the past.

2

Francine was quick to take advantage of the dry spell when the rain finally stopped to get out into the garden and trim back the rambling rose over the side trellis. She was holding the shears above her head and stretching for a tall errant offshoot when her mother stepped out of her room onto the terrace.

'Fancy a cup of tea in about five minutes?' Agnes called. 'I need to talk to you.'

'Please. There's a lemon drizzle cake in the tin if you fancy a slice.' Francine glanced across at Agnes but she had already disappeared back indoors. Cutting away at the lower, overgrown tangle of rose offshoots Francine's thoughts wandered to worries about Agnes. It was several years since there had been that stressed tone to her mother's voice. Definitely not since she and Edwin had moved into Francine's childhood home to live with Agnes fourteen months ago now. Was she ill? Maybe the results of a recent blood test had come back and there was a problem. Please no. The thought of her mother being ill made Francine herself feel bad. Gathering the cuttings into a green garden waste bag she dragged it up the garden towards the gate ready for Edwin to dispose of it.

Agnes carried the tea tray with its flowery china cups and saucers, slices of lemon cake on matching plates out to the terrace and sat waiting for her. Before joining her mother Francine went into the kitchen to wash her hands. The rinsed sherry glass on the draining board surprised her. Four o'clock in the afternoon and Agnes had been drinking? Something must have seriously upset her.

Agnes poured the tea as Francine sat on the wrought iron chair with its scarlet cushion. 'Lovely to be able to sit out here again. I think spring has finally arrived after all the rain,' Francine said. 'Shame it didn't arrive in time for Easter. So, what do you need to talk to me about, Maman?' she asked before taking a sip of tea and swallowing. 'Is it your blood test results?'

'*Non.* They are good.' Agnes muttered something under her breath in rapid French which Francine couldn't quite make out, and her heart sank. Agnes had a habit of reverting to her native French whenever stressed or agitated over something. Whatever she needed to talk about was clearly serious. Francine waited.

'Uncle Theo rang me this afternoon.'

'How is he?' Francine was very fond of her uncle Theo. He'd been very kind to her down the years on the numerous occasions she'd met him.

'He's well. He rang about your father,' Agnes said quietly.

'Like he couldn't ring himself,' Francine said.

'In this case he couldn't. He's had an accident.'

At the look on her mother's face, Francine stopped herself from making another sarcastic comment. Seeing Agnes take a deep breath, Francine knew instantly why she'd needed a drink that afternoon.

'He's dead, isn't he?'

Agnes nodded. 'Yes.'

Francine stayed silent, trying to assess her own feelings. Her father was dead. The father she barely knew; the father she'd not seen since she turned eighteen, thirty-six years ago. Her childhood memories of when he had been in her everyday life had faded, distorted, into unreliable pictures of her time growing up in France before the word 'separation' and all its consequences had become a presence in her life. She looked at Agnes.

'*Ça va*, Maman?' Francine asked gently. What was Agnes thinking? Her marriage might have ended many years ago but there was bound to be some sort of instinctive gut reaction to the news. Francine suspected it would be similar to her own – indifference – but in her mother's case, it would be laced with bitterness. She knew her mother well enough to know that the love between her parents, if in fact it had even existed in the beginning, had died a long time ago with Agnes ending up hating Oscar Agistini. Even if she had tried for years to hide that hate from her daughter. Agnes's lifelong maxim had always been 'the past is past, it's the future we need to worry about'.

Francine was close to her mother these days but she knew little about her life before the two of them had arrived in England. Agnes had always been one to keep private things to herself. The way people poured out their innermost thoughts on social media was unthinkable and abhorrent to her. 'I was brought up to smile at the world and hide any grief I might be experiencing.' It was a moral code drummed into Francine from an early age. One that she herself had unconsciously adopted and now, like Agnes, lived by.

Agnes nodded and muttered a quiet, '*Ça va, merci*. I am happy that it is finally over. Theo offered to ring and tell you but I thought you needed to hear the news from me.'

'How did he die?'

'Theo said it seems he had a heart attack as he was leaving his boat in the marina after an evening of drinking with another man and he fell between his boat and its neighbour. He died before he could be pulled out.'

'Will you go to the funeral?'

'*Non.*' Agnes said sharply, shaking her head.

'Do you think I should go?' Francine asked.

Agnes glanced at her, surprised. 'Do you want to?'

'No. But maybe Theo would appreciate one or both of us being there.'

'I will ask him when he rings with the details.' Agnes paused. 'Jasmine will need to be told.' As always, she called her granddaughter by her full name rather than by her preferred version, Zazz, that she'd insisted on using since secondary school.

'I'll phone her later. Oscar might have been her grandfather but as he's never been in her life, I doubt the fact that he's dead is going to affect her.'

'Such a difficult man,' Agnes muttered.

Francine nodded. Of all the words she could think of to describe her father – difficult was probably the politest and least offensive. Bully, mean-spirited, arrogant, tyrant, the list went on. He was all of those things and more. Francine remembered the last time she'd spoken to him, about nine months ago. Ironically the two of them shared a birthday and it had been the evening of her fifty-third birthday and his eighty-fourth...

Francine, Edwin and Agnes had been celebrating at a favourite restaurant when her mobile rang. She'd been tempted not to answer it. Zazz, who had gone to Ibiza with a couple of girlfriends for a long weekend break had rung her earlier to wish her Happy Birthday, and there was no-one else likely to ring her. But they were between courses so she gave it a quick glance. Unusually, it was Oscar's name showing on caller ID. Hesitantly Francine accepted the call and said 'Hello.'

Loud background noise told of a party in full swing. The words 'Happy Birthday' may have been uttered but were impossible to understand if they were. Oscar had been drunk, his words slurred and incoherent as he shouted into the phone. In the end Francine had hung up without being able to get in a word. Conversation with a sober Oscar was always difficult, with a drunken Oscar it was impossible...

That phone call had been as unexpected as it was unwelcome and Francine felt sure there was an unknown ulterior motive behind it, although it was one she'd been unable to discover so far. Now he was dead she was unlikely to ever know the truth behind the reason for the phone call.

Francine stood up and began to place cups and saucers back on the tray. 'I need to start dinner.'

'I'll come and give you a hand,' Agnes said.

As the two of them returned to the kitchen, they heard the front door close.

'Edwin's home,' Francine said, a note of relief in her voice. 'I think I'll ask him to phone Zazz.'

3

_____

It was mid-afternoon the next day when Theo rang with details of the funeral. But it turned out that there would be no funeral. Instead, there was to be a Direct Cremation without any attendees, the day after tomorrow. Apparently, Theo told them, it was the way to do things these days, especially when there were few, or no family relatives or mourners.

'I hope I do the right thing by agreeing to this,' Theo said. 'I do not think either of you would want to come for a funeral. And with the French law of cremation or burial having to take place within six days of death I wasn't sure you could both drop everything and come over within the next few days.' Theo paused.

'Definitely done the right thing,' said Edwin, who had joined them to hear the details.

Agnes released a relieved sigh. No funeral to attend and no mention of holding a memorial service, or heaven forbid, a last farewell party sometime in the future.

'Although the two of you might like to start to plan a visit for some time in the next week or two.'

'Truly? Why?' Francine asked.

'French wills are notoriously complicated. The notaire has requested a meeting with me tomorrow,' Theo continued, seemingly ignoring her question. 'As Oscar's nominated next of kin there are certain things I'm legally required to do. I'll know more about that after I've met with the notaire.'

When the call finished a few moments later, Francine turned to her mother. 'I don't understand why Theo thinks we should start to plan a visit, do you?'

Agnes shook her head and regarded Francine steadily for several seconds before giving an almost imperceptible sigh. 'You were our only child so as such, I expect you to inherit the bulk of Oscar's estate. It is impossible to disinherit one's children in France. I'd guess there are one or two "Oscar" conditions woven into you inheriting everything that the notaire needs to explain to you.'

Both Edwin and Francine stared at her.

'Are you saying that I have probably inherited the old family home in Le Suquet, Cannes? The house where we lived before coming here?' Her voice faded away as Agnes smiled and gave her a nod that answered her questions.

'Yes, the house and possibly everything else, except for perhaps a couple of bequests that Oscar may have made to a few individuals. Like Theo said, French wills can be very complicated. But I suspect he's right. We may well have to go to France.'

'Do you think he will have left you some money? I mean, I know he barely paid you a penny in maintenance all the years I was growing up. I know too how hard you had to work to feed us both, keep a roof over our heads. You're entitled to something now surely, out of his estate? How do you feel about me inheriting whatever it happens to be. Money? The house?'

Agnes gave a strangled laugh. 'I feel nothing. It's a house I lived in at a difficult time in my life and the good memories have been drowned out by the bad. As for accepting money from him,' she shook her head. 'I never wanted anything from him, especially after I'd left. The only thing I ever wanted from that life was you.'

'As his ex wife I still think you are entitled to something from his estate,' Francine said stubbornly. 'And if I can, I shall do my best to make sure you get something.'

'I truly don't need or want anything. I'm only sorry I didn't think to warn you about how strict the French are about following their inheritance laws.'

'To say it has come as a bit of a shock, is to put it mildly,' Francine said, rubbing her forehead. Her phone rang at that moment. Zazz.

'Hi darling, how are you?'

'Fine. Dad said when he rang to tell me about Oscar that Theo was dealing with the arrangements for the funeral. Do you know when it is yet?'

'Theo has arranged a Direct Cremation,' Francine said quietly. 'That way nobody has to worry about travelling to France in a hurry.'

'What do you mean? Aren't you and Granny going to go?' Zazz interrupted. 'I mean, I know there was no love lost between the three of you but he's dead.' Her voice rose on a hysterical note. 'How about paying your respects for god's sake?'

'How dare you.' Francine took a deep breath. 'Just when did you get so righteous and sanctimonious? And to be clear – I didn't have any respect for him when he was alive, so I have no intention of being a hypocrite and attending a funeral to pretend a respect I never felt for him. And I'm sure I'm speaking for Granny in this instance too.'

Silence. Francine took the phone away from her ear and looked at it.

'Zazz has hung up on me.' She turned to look at Edwin, a frown on her face. 'What the hell has got into our daughter? Oscar has never been in her life and now she wants to pay her respects as if he's been the perfect grandfather to her?'

Later that evening as she lay in bed trying to read and unable to concentrate, Agnes found herself thinking about Jasmine and her reaction to her unknown grandfather's death. Francine had spoken nothing but the truth, telling her that it would be hypocritical for the two of them to go and pay their false respects. Personally, she couldn't now remember a time when she had even liked Oscar, let alone respected him. As for love – if that was what her feelings for Oscar had ever been, they'd disappeared quicker than snowflakes in sunshine. She couldn't recall either that he had ever uttered the words 'I love you' to her. Agnes's mind drifted back to the beginning of her relationship with Oscar all those years ago...

She remembered being flattered by his attention. Ten years older than her, he had introduced her to a life she'd known existed on the Riviera but had never been a part of before. Oscar took her to the casinos in Juan-les-Pins, Nice and Monaco. He took her to balls in Monte Carlo and dances at the Hôtel de Provençal on several occasions, where she was awestruck by the famous people she saw there: Josephine Baker, an elderly Maurice Chevalier, Brigitte Bardot, Ella Fitzgerald, so many celebrities. She'd never forgotten the night he took her to the premiere of The Umbrellas of Cherbourg *at the Palais des Festivals in Cannes. She'd been a huge Catherine Deneuve fan ever since.*

But she knew that whilst she enjoyed the social life he'd introduced her to, she couldn't see their relationship lasting. He was too old-fash-

ioned in many ways; believed that women should defer to men. Once when she'd said how much she'd have liked to have gone to university, to have gained a degree, he'd smiled and said, 'A woman's place is in the home.' The flash of anger that crossed his face when she'd retorted, 'It's the 1960s not the dark ages,' had scared her, as well as his refusal to discuss his attitude towards the 'Women's Lib' movement that was sweeping through Europe.

Her parents though, had liked Oscar, said he was 'such a gentleman', and encouraged their relationship, saying that they knew she was safe when she was out with him. They dismissed her fears about his old-fashioned views of women saying he'd brought stability into her life and would look after her when they were gone. More importantly, her parents were determined that she was not going to follow in her elder sister, Denice's footsteps and bring shame on the family by running away to Paris to become an actress. After that conversation Agnes decided that the very next time she went out with Oscar she was going to tell him it was the last time. She didn't want to 'do a Denice' as her father had put it and run away to become an actress but neither did she want to spend the rest of her life with Oscar. Ironically that was the very night he chose to propose.

He'd booked a table at the Hôtel de Provençal in Juan-les-Pins for one of their regular dinner dances and had been extra solicitous about her welfare all evening. 'Was the meal to her liking? Would she like to dance? Did she want some more wine?' It was between courses after she'd declined to dance saying that she needed to talk to him that, at her words, Oscar unexpectedly dropped on to one knee and took hold of her hand. The chatter in the restaurant quietened as the band switched to a slow romantic beat.

Agnes froze. Please no. He couldn't be about to do what she thought he was? Had he sensed what she was going to say to him? Had he deliberately chosen such a public place, knowing that she was unlikely to cause a scene by refusing him? She trembled as Oscar pushed the *three stone diamond ring that had belonged to his mother onto her finger before she could snatch her hand back. She must have breathed the word 'No', because his face darkened with anger and he squeezed her hand in a vice-like grip. 'Marry me?'*

Tears that everyone took for tears of happiness were running down her face as she mutely nodded and Oscar stood up. Champagne arrived at their table, couples began congratulating them, her parents appeared. The presence of her parents told Agnes everything. They'd known this was going to happen and had given Oscar their blessing.

As soon as they were alone, she'd take off the ring and give it back. Tell him in no uncertain way that she couldn't marry him. Only of course, saying no to Oscar proved to be an impossible task and the most he would agree to was a six-month engagement. Agnes consoled herself with the thought that in that time she would be able to break it off...

She smothered a sigh. Clearly the news of his death had stirred up memories from deep in her brain. The next few weeks were going to be difficult and likely to bring even more memories she wished she didn't have to the surface. She fingered the Celtic necklace around her neck that these days she rarely took off. She had to trust that it would all come right in the end.

4

Zazz stomped her way around her local park, furious with herself. She shouldn't have pushed her mother so hard about the funeral. And she definitely shouldn't have hung up on her. It wasn't as if she didn't know Francine, like Agnes, had zero patience regarding Oscar. Never mentioning his name if they could avoid doing so, never talking to her about him even though he was – had been – her only living grandfather.

As for this non-funeral business. It wasn't that she was sanctimonious as her mother had called her, or even religious, she simply found it sad and upsetting that no-one cared enough to attend the final disposition of another human being.

The fact that both her mum and gran had assumed she wouldn't find the news upsetting because she had never met Oscar was wrong. She did find the news upsetting. She knew he was an old man who had made more enemies than friends during his life but he'd still been her grandfather even if they had never been allowed to meet. Both her parents and grandmother had always stressed the four of them were a family and as a family they would always care for each other – but Oscar was certainly not considered a part of their small family. *Persona non grata* was the phrase that summed him up in their family.

Down through the years this lack of communication with the French side of her family had built up a mountain of resentment in Zazz. She was half French for goodness' sake, she was entitled to know about her heritage, even if it turned out not to be one to be proud of. Her grandfather surely couldn't be that horrible. There had been times growing up when she'd longed to meet him. Her parents had taken her to France on several occasions during her childhood. Camping holidays on islands off the Atlantic coast, a Provençal gite with its lavender fields, the Loire Valley with its châteaux and once they'd spent almost a week in Paris. All happy memories of French family holidays but not one of them had been spent in the South of France. Zazz had never dared to rock the boat by asking why they couldn't go to the Riviera, knowing it would upset both her mother and grandmother.

Buying a coffee from the small wooden cafe hut in the park, Zazz sat on a nearby bench and thought about her future. The new life she planned to kick-start this summer was one which she'd discussed with nobody, including her mother and father. Or even her boyfriend, Rufus. On her own she'd weighed up the pros and the cons, done her due diligence as her dad would have urged her to do, saved some money – enough to live on for nine months – and decided the time was right to go for it. If it was a gigantic mistake she was young enough to pick up the pieces of her life and begin again. But she was confident it would work out well.

The day she'd told Iris, her flatmate, that she was moving out in a couple of weeks, was also the day she'd handed in her notice at the small digital publishing company in Bath where she'd worked for the last year. Marcus, her immediate boss, had initially tried to persuade her to stay but had ended up wishing her good luck and telling her to stay in touch.

Yesterday had been her last day in work and Iris's new flat-mate was moving in on Monday. Thankfully, as the furnished flat belonged to Iris there was only her personal stuff to pack into a large suitcase. Her immediate needs, including her laptop, passport, phone went into a rucksack. So, in theory, everything had slotted into place for her to begin her new life. She'd go home as she'd planned, spend some time with her parents and granny, Agnes, and tell the three of them all about her plans for the future, reassure them that yes, she did know what she was doing. And then simply go sometime next week.

Before then she had to talk to Rufus and tell him her plans, plans she'd deliberately kept from him too for several reasons. The main one being she had no idea how he would react to their current relationship becoming even more sporadic than it had been for the past nine months or so – ever since she'd decided to become a social media influencer. She'd been so busy trying to build up all her social media platforms, Instagram, Bluesky, her lifestyle blog and now her YouTube channel, ready for all of them to contribute to her earnings in her new life, that she'd cancelled several dates with him.

Zazz watched as a couple of magpies on the path in front of her squabbled and fought noisily over a crust of bread until one beak yanked it away from the other beak and it broke into two pieces. Triumphant, one bird flew away with its prize to a nearby oak tree.

Why did she feel so unsettled? Grandfather Oscar's unexpected demise would merely serve to disrupt things initially but, as sad as she found it, it was unlikely to have any real impact on her own life after so many years of being kept at arm's length. Impossible now to become closer to a grandfather she'd been kept away from but easier in many ways to accept his death because of the lack of personal memories.

5

Francine, still upset at the way Zazz had hung up on her, was grateful to Edwin when he suggested the three of them went down to their favourite riverside local restaurant for a meal that evening.

Sitting there sipping a glass of chardonnay, waiting for their meals and watching the activity on the river through the restaurant's huge picture window, Francine thought about how much their lives had changed in the last fourteen months or so. Edwin's redundancy had been the catalyst for them selling the house in Bath and, at Agnes's suggestion, joining her in the large Victorian terraced house in Dartmouth that she'd run as a busy guest house for years and where Francine had spent the majority of her childhood.

'I rattle around in it now I have virtually closed and only have the occasional guest from the old days,' Agnes had said. 'There is plenty of room for us all to live separate lives together.' She hadn't mentioned she'd welcome the company but Francine had quickly realised that was an important underlying part of the offer. Agnes was lonely.

The suggestion had been totally unexpected and would undoubtedly solve a major problem for them, but Francine had hesitated at first. Being Agnes's only child Francine had always known that her family home in Dartmouth would eventually pass to her. She and Edwin had even tentatively talked about moving down to be closer to Agnes as she grew older and even retiring there one day in the distant future but redundancy was not retirement. There was still at least a decade of working to get through before that happened.

Francine and Edwin debated for some time about Agnes's suggestion. Would accepting the offer be the right thing for them both in the long term? Edwin and Agnes had always got on but few men were likely to relish the thought of living with their mother-in-law. Edwin had simply shrugged when Francine had asked him how he felt about it.

'I don't see it being a problem. Like Agnes said, the house is plenty big enough for the three of us, it's a real family-sized house, so there's also room for Zazz if she decides to come with us, although I suspect she'll want to stay in Bath.' So the decision had been made. Sell up and move in with Agnes.

Even though Francine had been happy at the thought of 'going home' she was sad to leave Bath and the home she had loved. They'd been so lucky to find the 'Old Vicarage' twenty-five years ago long before the developers had started pulling down neighbouring houses with their large gardens and building two, if not three, houses on the plots. Surrounded now by a new small 'desirable' housing estate, the house with its classic Victorian design and large garden was something of a rarity in the neighbourhood. Something they found to be in their favour when they decided to sell up.

Edwin's redundancy package was generous after twenty years with the company but the thought of an uncertain income loomed large in her thoughts for weeks, months. At fifty-five Edwin was at the wrong end of the employment scale and was determined to work for himself this time. Although a well-respected graphic designer with lots of contacts in the industry, would any of them want to take him on as a freelancer? She, personally, as a copy editor and proofreader, could live and work anywhere in the county. But to have both of them relying on erratic freelance incomes would be a worry.

Now, fourteen months later everything had settled down. In many ways the twenty-five years that Francine had lived elsewhere had faded away as she settled back into the small town life she had grown-up with. Several of her old school friends who had married local men and still lived locally welcomed her back and soon she and Edwin's social lives were as busy as they'd ever been. Edwin had picked up several freelance design jobs, become a volunteer at the museum and was generally living a happier, stress-free life. Francine's money worries stilled once the money from the sale of the Bath house was safely in the bank along with the redundancy monies.

Francine's own work had continued uninterrupted, and she was as busy as she'd ever been. The manuscript currently on her desk in her office at the top of the house needed to be finished and returned by the day after tomorrow and she still had fifty pages to go before she could do a final read through. She'd prioritise it tomorrow, finish it and send it back so she'd be ready to go to France immediately if it was confirmed her and Agnes's presence was necessary. Ironically the book was one expanding on the joys of living on the River Dart in Devon, the very river she'd grown up alongside and was currently sitting by.

Always a busy port, these days it boasted two or three marinas and its deep safe harbour was popular with private yacht owners.

The jolly tune of 'I Do Like to Be Beside to Seaside' unexpectedly burst forth from Agnes's handbag making Francine shake her head and laugh as Agnes answered it.

'*Salut*, Theo. You have news?'

The waitress arrived with their meals at that moment and Francine missed hearing the beginning of her mother's conversation but she didn't miss the fleeting expression of concern that crossed her face. Two minutes later, as Agnes finished the call, Francine glanced across at her and waited while her mother took a sip of her wine.

'The notaire has cancelled Theo's meeting with him tomorrow and re-arranged it for the end of next week.'

'Did he give Theo a reason?'

'He has an unexpected court case to attend for one of his clients and next week is the first available time he can fit Theo in. He did apologise but said as the Agistini case is a non-urgent family one he hoped the delay would not inconvenience Theo too much. Theo said he had no option but to agree.' Agnes took another sip of her wine before giving Francine a serious look.

'But the notaire has also requested that you, me and Jasmine too, are at that meeting because of a complication he has found concerning the will.'

'The three of us need to go to France?' Francine said, puzzled. 'Why on earth would that be necessary? I can understand you and me, but Zazz too?'

'Theo, he thinks Jasmine is probably mentioned in the will,' Agnes shrugged. 'He said the notaire wouldn't discuss it over the phone but assured him it was a normal French inheritance complication. He simply wants to make sure everyone understands the implications of everything.'

'How do you feel, Maman, about returning to France after all this time?'

Agnes bit her lip. 'It will be easier knowing that Oscar is not going to make his presence felt, that's certain but,' she shrugged. 'I can't begin to think what it will be like to be honest, although hopefully it will finally draw a veil over the past for me, so there could be something good in that respect.'

'Going *en famille* will help too, I think,' Francine said. 'I'll phone Zazz when we get home. She did say she'd arrange some time off when she thought there would be a funeral to attend, so I'm sure it won't be a problem for her.'

Agnes barely registered Francine's words, suddenly lost in her own thoughts about the ordeal ahead of her in the next week or two. How on earth could she circumnavigate her way around the unknown problems that were on the horizon? Oscar might be dead but this complication with his will was sure to cause her difficulties and mess with her head like he had in the past. She could practically see that familiar smug, cruel smile on his lips as he'd planned this final upset to her life. Would she be able to draw a veil over her past like she had said to Francine? Perhaps, although she couldn't help thinking that people might die, but their cruel actions remained forever as memories.

* * *

Returning home after their meal, Edwin went upstairs to the room he'd turned into his office saying he wanted to finalise a quotation for a website he'd been asked to design. Agnes said she was going to watch TV in the sitting room and Francine, hoping that Zazz would be in a better frame of mind, made for the kitchen to ring her.

'Once I've spoken to Zazz, I'll come and join you,' she told Agnes.

Zazz answered her phone warily. 'Hi Mum. I was going to ring you later. I'm sorry about hanging up on you. I know I was rude.'

'You were,' Francine said. 'Unexpectedly and completely without cause – not like you at all. Have things gone wrong at work or something? Is it Rufus?'

'No, Rufus and everything is fine,' Zazz answered quickly. 'It was just the shock of Oscar's death and I'd not heard Direct Cremations were an actual thing before. I find it incredibly upsetting that there are people out there who apparently have no-one to mourn them.'

'I'm sure there are wakes or memorial services held after the event for the majority of deceased people,' Francine said, before falling silent for a second or two. 'Theo rang this evening. The notaire has asked for a meeting to discuss the will at the end of next week. He has also requested that as well as Granny and I being there that you attend too. Can you get the time off work? Maybe a week?'

'Getting time off work isn't a problem,' Zazz said quickly. 'I was coming down to stay for a few days anyway.'

'Okay. I'll book tickets and we can sort out the details when you're here.'

'See you soon then.' And Zazz ended the call.

Francine joined Agnes in the sitting room. 'Zazz is coming home for a few days and is okay to come to France with us as well. Tomorrow I'll find flights and book the tickets.' She collapsed onto the settee with a yawn. 'Life does like to shake things up at times, doesn't it?' she said, a rueful tone to her voice.

Agnes nodded but didn't answer. She had no intention of telling Francine that she suspected this particular shake up would very likely prove to be calamitous for their little family in more ways than one.

6

The morning of Oscar's cremation Agnes sat out in the garden deep in thought, half listening to the dawn chorus and watching the sky turn blue as the sunrise with its pink and red overtones faded away when the sun was fully risen. She remembered so many mornings she'd sat out here down through the years; some-times psyching herself up to get on with the way her life as it was and other, better times, sitting and simply enjoying the early morning quiet before she began her busy day. Today was not a psyching-herself-up kind of day. It was more a deep-breath-of-relief kind of day; relief that she had given up ever hoping to feel. She had to hold on firmly to the knowledge that she had Francine, the pride and joy of her life and now she was finally free of Oscar, the biggest mistake of her life.

Her conversation with Theo late last night after Francine and Edwin had gone to bed drifted into her mind. Dear Theo, her greatest supporter down the years against his own brother. As brothers went they were chalk and cheese, good versus evil. Having Theo in her life, even at a distance most of the time, had meant so much to her. She'd been hoping that Theo would be able to tell her more than he'd said in his earlier phone call. Something that he might not have wanted her to tell Francine. But for once he'd failed to reassure her, insisting that he had no more information.

'The notaire, he will tell us everything,' he kept repeating. 'It is better that way.' There was a pause before he continued.

'I am looking forward to the three of you being here next week,' he said quietly. 'Even though I know it will be *très difficile* for you returning after such a long absence. For Francine and Zazz not so much, but I hope you know I will help you all in whatever ways I can.'

Agnes had murmured her thanks before quietly saying good-night and ending the call. She'd been left with the strong impression that Theo did know more than he was admitting but for some obscure reason was not prepared to confide in her as he would normally. They'd been so close once...

She and Oscar had been engaged a couple of weeks, when Theo returned to Cannes after a band tour that had taken him all over Europe. As brothers the two of them couldn't have been more different in either looks or personality. Oscar, as the elder brother, had inherited the family property business. A prosperous well-established business that continued to thrive for several years under his control. Theo, a talented musician who played both the piano and the saxophone, was part of a successful rock band and was away performing for months at a time. His life at the time was a nomadic one and Oscar made no secret of the fact that he was of the opinion it was time his younger brother grew up and found a proper job.

Agnes quickly realised how much she liked Theo. How much more she had in common with him than with Oscar. Theo lit up the room for her as soon as he entered in a way that Oscar failed to do. Nearer her age than Oscar, the two of them quickly developed a strong friendship. Agnes even found herself wishing that she was marrying Theo. A thought she quickly pushed away, determining to tell Oscar again she didn't want to marry him and break off their engagement. The first time she tried to give him the ring back, he'd just looked at her and said, 'Don't be silly.' Somehow she had to make him understand she meant what she said. She also vowed to spend less time with Theo. Being accused of leading him on when she was engaged to his brother wasn't something she wanted to happen.

After a particularly boring evening with some of Oscar's friends, where she'd spent the time secretly planning to give him the ring back as he walked her home, another couple accompanied them most of the way and it was impossible to do or say anything. She stifled a sigh, she'd missed her opportunity again. Oscar turned to her as they said goodnight at the door of her parents' house.

'You have a busy month ahead. I have to go away for a week or two but I've decided on the date of our wedding, so you'll have lots to keep you busy and out of mischief. In a month's time you will become my wife. Your parents are pleased.' He gave her a quick kiss. 'Goodnight. Sleep well.' And he was gone before she could open her mouth to protest.

She stared after him, speechless. Why was everyone taking these decisions without her? What had happened to their six-month engagement? It was barely a month old. Why couldn't her parents have discussed it with her first? It was her life they were giving scant regard to. Didn't they care about her future happiness? All her father seemed to care about was marrying her off quickly to an outwardly successful man and basking in his status.

Agnes went indoors in a daze promising herself that she'd talk to her parents first thing in the morning. Surely they would listen and understand, if she put into words how worried she was about her impending marriage and how she didn't love Oscar and needed their help to break off the engagement. Even with their help she knew it would be difficult to stop this rollercoaster of a wedding. The one person she longed to talk to about it, Theo, and ask his advice, was of course an impossibility.

But it was stopping the wedding that would prove to be impossible.

7

After a fitful night's sleep Francine woke early and made her way down to the kitchen. She and Edwin had talked last night and decided there was little point in him going to France with them straight away. He had a couple of jobs to finish and then he'd fly over in a few days. Once in bed though sleep eluded her, her memory seemingly on a mission to remind her of things from the past she'd rather forget. Seeing Agnes out on the terrace she made two coffees and made her way outside.

'Good morning, Maman. How long have you been sitting out here?'

'I lose track of time,' Agnes said, gratefully accepting the mug Francine handed her. 'Did you sleep well?'

Francine shook her head. 'Too many memories floating around. Mainly that awful last summer visit when I had that major fallout with Oscar.' Even now, thirty-six years later, Francine could feel herself trembling at how awful it had been. Since then she'd never called him anything other than Oscar and had never been back to either Cannes or anywhere else in the South of France.

All communication between her and Oscar in the years following since then had been done via phone calls or e-mails and the occasional very short sessions on FaceTime. As Agnes gave her a worried look, Francine took a sip of her coffee and willed herself to be calm and stay in the moment. She'd never given Agnes the full details of what had happened on that dreadful day of her last summer holiday with her father, and she didn't intend to after all this time.

'I'll get on the computer when I've drunk this and book the tickets,' she said, bringing the conversation firmly back to the present. 'It will be just the three of us, Edwin is staying here to hold the fort and will join us in a few days. Shall we go out for lunch today? Totnes and Dartington Hall? A quick look around the grounds and then lunch at our favourite pub restaurant. Take our mind off things.'

Agnes nodded. 'Sounds good. Do you know what time Jasmine is arriving?'

'No. Late afternoon is her usual time.' Francine drained her coffee and stood up.

'I was wondering,' Agnes said quietly. 'What Theo is likely to do with the ashes when he collects them from the crematorium.'

Francine stilled. 'No idea. Throw them in the Med maybe? I don't suppose he'll want them on the mantelpiece. Right. I'll go and book the tickets and then I'll organise breakfast.'

Up in her office Francine quickly searched for and found available flights from Bristol to Nice on various days, chose an afternoon one and typed in her credit card details. It already felt strange knowing that in a few days she would be returning to the South of France and facing the memory of a life that barely registered in her brain these days but still occasionally surprised her with a painful jolt. And if she was feeling this way, goodness only knew how Agnes was truly feeling.

Waiting for the confirmation e-mail, her thoughts drifted back to Agnes's question about the ashes. What would Theo do with his brother's remains? Maybe it would be a good idea to have a small wake and then the four of them could dispose of Oscar's ashes in a suitable place to give everyone closure over the past and let them move on. Perhaps she'd suggest it when they were there, see how everyone else felt.

* * *

Zazz settled back in her seat with a sigh as she waited for the train to leave the station. Another few hours and she'd be home in Dartmouth. The last couple of days had been busy, not to mention difficult. Rufus had been less than understanding as she'd finally told him of her plans two nights ago, over supper in his favourite bistro. She knew she was in the wrong for not discussing them with him before but she'd had this idea in her head that once people knew they would try to dissuade her. It had been better to work it all out and present it as a *fait accompli*. Only Rufus didn't see it that way.

'I can't believe you've planned this secretly. Without even asking my advice. I thought we meant something to each other,' he'd said.

She sighed. The two of them had had fun in the last year. She liked Rufus a lot but the word *love* had not been uttered by either of them to the other. The phrase 'friends with benefits' had summed up their friendship perfectly. Zazz had never seen their relationship as permanent and she'd thought Rufus felt the same. Apparently not.

'You do mean something to me,' she said now. 'You're the first person I've told. I haven't even told my parents yet. I needed to work things out by myself. I didn't want anybody telling me it was a silly idea.'

'And now your silly idea means we're breaking up.'

'It's not a silly idea and, yes, I suppose we are breaking up – although we can remain friends. Keep in touch with each other – Facebook, WhatsApp, e-mails and once I'm settled you can come and visit. I'll be back to see you and my parents – I'm going to Europe, not Australia. Besides, your life is going to change in a few weeks when your current contract ends. Who knows where you'll end up.'

But Rufus had refused to be mollified. 'I can't believe you shut me out and organised a new life without consulting me. If you'd said and waited three months we could have gone travelling together. I'd never shut you out of my life like that.'

'But that's the whole point. I'm not going travelling. I'm going to live in one place. Live in the local French community. And I want to go now – not wait until your current work contract ends.' Zazz took a deep breath. Guiltily, she realised she had shut Rufus out, expecting him to understand the reasons why she'd acted like she had, which he clearly didn't. Possibly because she hadn't told him the full story. The real reason why she had kept her plans secret from everyone.

'Rufus, I'm sorry, I didn't mean to hurt or upset you but this is something I need to do for myself. Surely we can still be friends?' Silence had greeted her words.

The evening had ended with them barely speaking, Rufus placing a goodbye kiss on her cheek and grudgingly wishing her good luck before walking away. Saddened, Zazz had watched him go, hoping that he would eventually forgive her and their friendship would survive this blow she was guilty of dealing it. But if it didn't, then she'd have to accept that it wasn't meant to be.

As the train began to move Zazz gazed out of the window thoughtfully. The first foray into her new life was about to begin and her fingers were firmly crossed that all would be well.

8

Francine was in the kitchen on the phone giving Theo their travel details, as he'd insisted he would be at the airport to collect them, when Zazz arrived home. Francine smiled her welcome before finishing her conversation with Theo.

'Are you sure about meeting us? We can easily get a taxi and save you the trouble.' She smiled at something Theo said. 'Okay, we'll see you the day after tomorrow then, four o'clock at Nice airport. Thank you.' Ending the call, she turned to hug Zazz.

'Welcome home, darling. Big suitcase for a quick visit?'

Zazz returned the hug but ignored the question behind her words. 'Great to be home. Dad around?'

'It's his afternoon for volunteering at the museum. He'll be home in about an hour.'

'How's Granny coping with Oscar's death?'

'Difficult to say. She seems okay,' Francine said. 'Busy packing for our trip and hiding her true emotions away as usual.'

'We're good at doing that in this family,' Zazz said and immediately wished she'd kept her mouth closed when her mother threw her a look.

'And what exactly do you mean by that?' she demanded.

Zazz shrugged. 'Nothing in particular, it's just the way we are as a family. I'll take my stuff up to my room, and then find Granny to say hi. I'll help you with dinner later if you like,' and she quickly picked up her suitcase and rucksack and went upstairs before Francine could question her further.

Francine stayed where she was for a moment, wishing she knew what was bothering her daughter because there was definitely something going on, she'd not been her normal good-natured self for several months now. Maybe she'd suggest Agnes have a gentle probe to try and unearth what was wrong; she had always been able to coax Zazz's worries out of her. The three of them spending time together in France would be a good opportunity to talk too. The meeting with the notaire was the reason for the visit but there would surely be time for some exploring and relaxing, a mini holiday, after they'd got the will business out of the way. She'd booked flexible tickets so they could stay on for as long as they needed or wanted.

Francine heard Zazz coming downstairs and going out to the terrace where Agnes was sitting reading and enjoying the sun. Standing by the kitchen window she saw Zazz hug and kiss her gran before sitting down with her. Agnes laid her book aside and Francine suppressed a sigh as she watched the two of them begin to chat animatedly.

When was the last time she and Zazz had sat down together like that and chatted? Not the last time she was home, or the time before. She forced her mind back and realised that since they'd left Bath and moved to Dartmouth, Zazz had only been home a handful of times and then only briefly. She hadn't even managed a visit for her last birthday, just a short phone call, which had upset Francine at the time but she'd accepted the apology and the beautiful silk scarf Zazz had gifted her without commenting.

After all Zazz was twenty-three now, an independent woman with a busy life, she was entitled to spend time away with her friends. Turning away from the window Francine determined that when they were in France she would make a concentrated effort to try and repair her and Zazz's fractured mother-daughter relationship.

* * *

The evening before they left for France the four of them enjoyed a fish and chip supper that Edwin had insisted on treating them to. Zazz had volunteered to go and collect their food from their favourite takeaway and they ate sitting out on the garden terrace, albeit with their fleeces on, enjoying the cool evening air.

'I'm glad you're going with your mum and granny,' Edwin said. 'And that you didn't have a problem getting time off work.'

Zazz briefly thought about telling everyone about giving her notice in but knowing that her mother would instantly bombard her with questions, decided against it. Instead she smiled at her dad. 'I was due some leave,' she said, which was true in a way. 'Shame you're not coming to France with us. It would have been our first family holiday in the South of France.'

'Dad will be joining us later. If Oscar hadn't died we wouldn't be going. It's not as if we've been planning a holiday down there,' Francine said. 'I suspect it's going to be a difficult few days for Maman, and probably myself,' she muttered under her breath.

She glanced at Edwin. 'I know you said you had a few things scheduled to finish in the next week but you can change your mind and come with us instead of waiting until later.'

'Let's see how long it takes to sort things out,' Edwin said easily. 'Agnes has always told us how convoluted French bureaucracy can be. In the meantime I'm sure the three of you will have some time to relax and...' he paused. 'Make some happier memories for Agnes and yourself,' he said, looking at Francine. He turned to Zazz. 'Whilst you, young lady, can enjoy your first visit to the French Riviera.'

Zazz wriggled in her seat. To say she was beginning to feel uncomfortable was an understatement. She wasn't exactly lying but she knew her dad could accuse her of lying by omission. She'd planned on coming home to tell them everything this week so why didn't she just open her mouth and speak? Because she knew that her mother and grandmother were not going to take kindly to her news when she did pluck up the courage to tell them. No, best wait until they were in France and her secret plan of moving there was already partly implemented.

9

Agnes searched the crowds waiting to greet friends and family in the Arrivals Hall at Nice airport, anxiously looking for Theo's familiar face. He wasn't difficult to spot, at six feet three inches he often stood head and shoulders above any crowd even if those shoulders were a little bent these days. She spotted him almost instantly, standing apart from the crowd with a dog sitting patiently at his feet. A smile broke over both their faces as the two of them saw each other and Agnes immediately relaxed. Being with Theo was always good, they shared so much life history since meeting all those years ago.

Once all the normal hugs and kisses were out of the way Theo introduced Cerise the dog, whom Zazz was already petting having dropped down onto her knees.

'She was Oscar's dog so I've looked after her since the accident,' Theo said, a rueful smile on his face. 'Impossible to let her go to the refuge. She's not a problem which given her sad history is remarkable, but I never have a dog before.'

'She seems taken with Zazz,' Francine said, watching as

Cerise, her tail switching frantically, tried to climb on to Zazz's knees. 'What breed is she? And what's her sad history?'

'Tibetan terrier,' Theo answered. 'Oscar found her about nine months ago on the autoroute one night coming home from Nice. No collar, no chip.'

'She's adorable,' Zazz said. 'I suspect she will be missing Oscar.' She gave Cerise another stroke before standing up. 'Shall I take her,' and she held out her hand for the lead.

'*Bien*. Let us find the car and get you all back to Cannes,' Theo said, taking charge of the trolley with three cases and Zazz's rucksack loaded on it.

The sweet, almost medicinal, camphor smell of the tall eucalyptus trees surrounding the airport made Agnes catch her breath with delight. So many years since she'd inhaled that particular, once familiar, smell. Walking across to the car under a clear blue sky the heat in late April was already stifling in its intensity. Zazz helped Theo load the cases into the car as Agnes settled herself in the front passenger seat and Francine sat in the back. As Zazz swung her rucksack in on top of her case, Theo asked quietly. 'You tell them about what you did? And the other thing you plan?'

Zazz shook her head. '*Non.*' Quickly adding as Theo looked at her crossly. 'But I will soon, promise.'

'If you do not, then I will. The news will give them unhappiness but they deserve to know it.' And he closed the car door with barely controlled force.

Leaving the airport, Theo drove them along the bord de mer which was far busier than either Francine or Agnes remembered it being. The Mediterranean glistening on their left though was reassuringly the same; the beaches dotted with parasols and windbreakers but not as crowded as in July and August.

Forty minutes later, as they passed The Palm Court onto the

beginning of the Croisette in Cannes, Theo looked in his rear-view mirror at Francine and Zazz before glancing across at Agnes sitting next to him in the front passenger seat.

'Agnes, you remember my house in the old town down by the harbour, I think you all like to stay with me there rather than in,' he hesitated. 'Rather than in Oscar's house at the top of Le Suquet.'

Agnes nodded gratefully. '*Merci.* I would prefer to stay with you.'

Francine, knowing how much her maman had been dreading going back to the house she'd shared all those years ago with Oscar, breathed a sigh of relief. It meant she didn't have to stay there either. She opened her mouth to accept Theo's offer but Zazz was already speaking.

'If nobody minds, I'd rather like to stay in Oscar's house,' Zazz said, cuddling Cerise who had climbed onto her lap and refused to budge. 'Happy to take this one with me too.'

Silence followed her words. Theo, about to say that was fine, caught a glimpse of Francine's face in the mirror and stayed silent.

Francine stared at her daughter before saying. 'Thanks for the offer, Theo, but I'll go to Oscar's with Zazz.'

'I know it will be hard for you to stay in the house so please don't bother on my behalf,' Zazz protested. 'I don't need company.'

'I know but I'm still staying in that house with you.'

'Whatever,' Zazz said before shrugging and turning to look out of the window.

'I have an idea,' Theo said breaking the uncomfortable silence that descended. 'We park the car and go to my house, maybe a cup of coffee or have a glass of wine and then the three of us will walk up the back way to Oscar's. Agnes can have a rest if she needs it before we go out for dinner this evening.'

'Sounds like a plan,' a tight-lipped Francine muttered.

Ten minutes later, after parking the car down on the harbour, Theo led them the two or three hundred metres or so across the main road and into a labyrinth of narrow roads lined with tall old houses built in elevated positions overlooking the old harbour before stopping in front of a bright yellow door at the end of a terrace.

'*Bienvenue chez moi*,' Theo said, unlocking the door and ushering them in. The downstairs of the old fisherman's cottage had been converted and modernised sympathetically into an open-plan living and kitchen area. French doors at the end opened onto an outdoor area where a well-established, thick-trunked bougainvillea, its magenta bracts vivid in the sunshine, could be seen. Terracotta tiles on the floor, cream walls with blue and yellow Provencal splashback tiles in the kitchen area above the sink and the marble worktops. Cream curtains with a green olive print hung beneath the worktops hiding shelves and basket containers, with an under-the-counter fridge on the end. The range-type cooker was positioned near the window. A breakfast bar with more curtained shelves on the kitchen side separated the kitchen from the remaining large comfortable dining and living area.

A table with four chairs, a squishy three-seater settee and a small coffee table stood in front of the inset log burner in the living area. A highly polished black Steinway upright piano was placed in front of one wall. Bookshelves packed tightly with books and the occasional ornament and framed photo, were fixed to every conceivable free wall space.

'This is lovely,' Agnes said, looking around appreciatively. 'You renovated it beautifully. I remember it was in terrible condition when you bought it. It's the kind of house I always imagined you living in.'

'*Merci*. I am happy here,' Theo smiled at her.

'I don't see your saxophone?' Agnes said, looking around.

'I only play the piano these days. I find I'm quite in demand in the summer for the old-fashioned afternoon tea dances that are gaining in popularity. *Bien*! Wine, tea or coffee?'

'Tea please,' Agnes and Francine said together.

'I'd prefer coffee,' Zazz said. 'But I'll have the same as everyone else.'

'Nespresso okay?' Theo pointed to his machine and Zazz moved towards it, nodding happily.

Her coffee pod quickly pressed through the machine, Zazz opened the door and took her cup out into the yard while Theo carried Agnes's case upstairs and showed her the room he thought she'd prefer. Francine organised three teas and brought them out and placed them on the wrought-iron table before sinking onto one of the chairs. Zazz sipped her coffee, hoping Agnes and Theo wouldn't be too long.

'Why are you so intent on staying in Oscar's house?' Francine asked quietly.

Zazz smothered a sigh. She knew she had to talk to her mother soon but she didn't want to start that conversation here when they would be interrupted – and possibly joined – by Agnes and Theo. 'Mum, there are a couple of things I need to tell you but can we talk later please? When we're alone.'

Francine stared at Zazz for several seconds before giving her a quick nod in agreement as the others joined them.

10

Half an hour later Theo took a key off a board hidden in a nook in the kitchen and turned to Francine and Zazz. 'Ready to walk up to the house?'

'I'm sure we can find it,' Francine said. 'I don't remember Le Suquet being that big so I may even recognise the way.'

Zazz opened her mouth about to agree with her mother but thought better of it.

Theo shook his head. 'I'll walk you up the short way this first time.' He bent down and clipped Cerise on her lead, which prompted a lot of wriggling and tail wagging from the happy dog, before he handed the lead to Zazz.

'Cerise and you can lead the way. I'll take your suitcase if you can manage the rucksack.'

'I'll sit outside and enjoy the sun whilst you're gone,' Agnes said, glad of the opportunity to be alone and collect her thoughts. Thoughts that were a mix of jumbled feelings. Did she feel happy being back in the South of France? Yes, she thought she did. But what problems lay ahead in the next day or two? How would she cope with those problems when they presented themselves, as

they surely would? One thing she did know though, she was glad
to be staying here with dear Theo and not having to brave her old
home, with its myriad of unhappy memories. Oscar might not
have a physical presence there any more but Agnes knew the air
would be full of him. She pushed away the thought that the
house would of course have to be faced one day in the near
future.

Sitting there in the peaceful courtyard, with the warmth of
the sun on her body, Agnes's thoughts drifted back once again to
the wedding she'd tried so desperately to stop...

*The morning after Oscar had sprung the surprise date for their
wedding on her, she'd tried to talk to her mum on her own. Woman to
woman. But her mother kept shaking her head. 'All we want is for you
to be taken care of. Be secure. Oscar has money, he will look after you.'*

*'But I don't love him and he doesn't truly love me either,' Agnes
protested.*

*'He wants to marry you. You are still underage. Whatever is your
father going to say if you break off your engagement?'*

*In the end Agnes gave up. She couldn't break through her mother's
lack of empathy with her situation. Her mother was of the wrong
generation. She deferred to her husband in everything. There was little
point in asking her to help talk to him. To stand at her side as she tried
to explain why she couldn't marry Oscar. More than anything she
wished she'd never met the man and cursed the day she'd accepted his
invitation to dinner because she felt flattered by his attention.*

*A serious-looking Theo had turned up mid-morning the next day
saying they needed to talk.*

*'What's happened to your eye?' she asked, looking at the multi-
coloured bruise surrounding it.*

'Oscar's fist,' Theo said.

'What! Why?'

'He didn't like me telling him he was bullying you into marrying

him. Told me that it was nonsense, it was none of my business and to butt out.'

'I'm so sorry.'

'You're not the one who hit me. Don't you dare apologise for my brother the bully.'

'He's brought the wedding forward because,' Theo grabbed hold of Agnes's hands, 'he knows how I feel about you. He doesn't love you but he doesn't want me to have you. You make a terrible mistake if you marry him. Please don't. Marry me instead.'

Agnes looked at him, stunned at his words.

'I love you, Agnes. I haven't told you before because I'd hoped the more we saw of each other you'd realise we belong together. I thought we had more time to get to know each other. I didn't expect Oscar to bring the wedding forward. You have to break off your engagement.'

'They won't let me,' Agnes whispered. 'I've tried. Papa, he is determined for me to marry Oscar.'

'I go speak to him. Tell him I want to marry you,' Theo said. 'If he say no, will you run away with me?'

Agnes closed her eyes. 'If between us we can persuade my parents to cancel this wedding then you and I can have a future together but I don't think I'm brave enough to run away with you.'

The closing of the front door as Theo arrived home brought Agnes out of her dream with a start.

11

Leaving the cottage, Theo led Francine and Zazz up a nearby flight of shallow steps and then along a street barely the width of a small car. Tall narrow houses dating from the days of the eighteenth century when Cannes was just a small insignificant Mediterranean fishing port lined both sides. Some of the houses looked vaguely familiar to Francine, but that could be simply because over the last decades she'd grown used to seeing the stereotypical images of houses in the South of France that the media favoured: rampant colourful bougainvillea covering pastel-painted walls and cats sleeping on window sills just like the ginger one that Cerise briefly inspected before receiving a sharp paw on her nose.

Noticing how happy Zazz was with Cerise trotting alongside her, Francine felt a twinge of guilt. Growing up, Zazz had frequently begged for a dog but the timing had never been right and she and Edwin had always refused. Although, if she were to be honest, there had been several times when Edwin had tried to make her change her mind as he'd grown up with a family dog and suggested it would be good for Zazz. Perhaps they should offer to give Cerise a home if Theo didn't want to keep her. Zazz would then get to see her at weekends. No, silly idea. Zazz wasn't home often enough these days. Cerise would end up being their dog.

At that moment Zazz and Cerise turned and disappeared down an adjoining narrow lane. Francine glanced at Theo. 'My sense of direction has gone haywire – is Zazz going the right way?'

'Cerise knows the way home.' Theo smiled at her and she nodded.

'Of course.'

'The house – it is not like it was when you and Agnes lived here,' Theo said quietly. 'Or even how it was during your summer visits. It is different now. A little neglected in places.'

Francine glanced at him, wondering what he meant but the moment was gone as they caught up with Zazz and Cerise who were waiting outside a sun-faded blue door. Francine caught her breath as she recognised it. Thirty-six years had passed since she'd last seen the door of the house Agnes had brought her home to from Cannes hospital. Theo unlocked the door and handed the key to Francine as they all walked inside.

'I am *désolé* I haven't prepared the beds here,' Theo said. 'I thought you stay with me.'

'No worries, we can do our own beds.' Francine's voice was quiet as the significance of where she was and what she was doing unexpectedly struck her.

'Are you okay?' Zazz said. 'You've gone pale. Why don't you go back to Theo's? I'll be fine here on my own.'

Francine shook her head. 'No. I'm staying. If nothing else it will be good to get the ghosts out of my head.' Sleeping ghosts that she could feel now stirring like demented devils.

Theo gave her an anxious glance. 'If you're sure. I've booked an early table – seven thirty – at the Auberge on rue Saint Antoine. Shall we meet there? Or do you want to come down to me first for an aperitif?'

'We'll meet you there,' Zazz said decisively without consulting her mother.

After Theo left, taking Cerise with him saying that he didn't want her unsettled by being back in her old home, Francine and Zazz took their cases upstairs.

'That was Oscar's room,' Francine said, pointing at the first door they came to. 'I don't expect either of us want to sleep in there. The bathroom is here, you can take the room next to it, if you like, and I'll have this one opposite. As I remember it, there is another bedroom up there,' and she pointed at a spiral staircase at the end of the hallway. 'But that may not be in use these days.' She opened the door she was standing next to and dragged her suitcase inside before Zazz could react.

Zazz walked to the end of the hallway, passing the large armoire placed against the wall halfway along, looked over her shoulder to check that Francine had closed her bedroom door and slowly climbed the spiral staircase with her luggage. The spacious attic room she stepped into was perfect with its beamed and sloping ceiling and windows that gave a glimpse of the Mediterranean. Sparsely furnished there was a large double bed, a chest of drawers, a hanging rail in the recess for a wardrobe, a small desk and a comfortable chair placed near the window. Zazz sighed happily before leaving her case and rucksack on the floor by the bed and turning to run lightly back down the spiral stairs. Opening the large armoire, she was pleased to see it full of towels as well as the bed linen she'd hoped to find and she began to pull out duvet covers, pillowcases and sheets. She grabbed a couple of towels but didn't bother pulling duvets down from the top shelf, it was warm enough to sleep under a simple cover.

Holding bed linen for Francine as well she moved towards the room her mother had chosen. 'I'll give you a hand making your bed, shall I?' Her voice faded away as she saw her mother sitting on the bed staring into space.

'Mum, what's wrong?'

Francine gave a start and stood up. 'Nothing is wrong. I just got caught up in memories of the past. You've found the bed linen, thanks,' and Francine held out her hands to take some.

'This is a nice room,' Zazz said.

Francine nodded. 'Yes, it's the room I usually stayed in as a teenager when I came for the mandatory daughter-father visits. The room you're in was my bedroom before, before Maman and I left.'

'I've decided to sleep up on the next floor,' Zazz said. 'It's still a bedroom and has a lovely view. Got to love climbing a spiral stair-case to go to bed. Come on, let's make up your bed,' she added before her mother could question her choice of room.

'Thank you.'

As Zazz straightened up a few minutes later after smoothing down the duvet cover she said. 'I think I'll unpack and then have a shower – unless you'd like first shower?'

'No, I'll have one after you. I might just lie on the bed and read my Kindle for a bit after I've unpacked.'

'I'll see you later then,' and Zazz pulled the door closed behind her as she left.

Up in the attic room Zazz quickly made the bed before unpacking and hanging her clothes on the rail in the recess and placing the rest of her stuff in the chest of drawers. Her laptop she placed on the desk and after sending Rufus a quick WhatsApp message to say she'd arrived she put her phone alongside it.

A few moments later and Zazz was in the surprisingly modern bathroom, standing under the rainfall power shower luxuriating in the feel of the hot water as it pounded away the tension that had gripped her shoulders all day. As she felt herself relax, she decided that tonight over dinner at the auberge would possibly be a good time to talk to her mother and grandmother with Theo there to help keep things calm. He'd been cross with her at the airport but hopefully he would be able to help her make both of them understand why she had done what she had. At least she hoped he would help, Zazz sensed he didn't entirely approve of her actions over the past few months. And he, like the others, didn't know the half of them so far and was equally unlikely to approve of them.

12

After Zazz left her, Francine sank back down on the now made bed and tried to rationalise her thoughts. However strange it felt to be back in Le Suquet and here in this house, she had to deal with it. Staying at Theo's would have been easier for there were no bad memories associated with it but letting Zazz come here to stay on her own had never been an option in her mind. At least Agnes had been spared the trauma of returning to the house she'd run away from nearly half a century ago. Francine closed her eyes and immediately the times she'd slept in this room in the past slipped into her mind...

How she'd hated leaving Agnes in the summer without help in the B&B and how Oscar smiled at her and raised his eyebrows in irritation every year when she mentioned it. She'd been twelve before Agnes finally gave in to Oscar's demands that she stayed with him for two weeks every summer and allowed her to go. So, for the next six years, there had been a summer pattern to her life.

Agnes always drove her up to Bristol airport, checked her in as an unaccompanied minor and saw her safely into the departure lounge before turning away and going home. Francine still remembered the taste of bile in her mouth that first time, how nauseous she'd felt as she watched Agnes walk away after telling her Oscar would be waiting for her at Nice. In the summers that followed, it was often Theo waiting to meet her because Oscar was busy with 'business'.

That first summer of travelling alone to France kickstarted a steep growing-up curve in her life. She didn't tell Agnes some of the things that happened in France knowing she wouldn't like it. Even at that young age she'd been sensitive to her mother's feelings and divided them into 'on a need-to-know basis' that wouldn't upset her mother. Most days she walked down through Cannes to see Theo who at the time was busy still renovating the old house he'd purchased a few years ago. Theo treated her like his favourite person in the world, he was always pleased to see her at any time. Oscar, even though it was he who insisted she came every summer, sometimes made her feel she got in his way and was a bit of a nuisance. She'd quickly realised after the first summer that Oscar was simply exercising his rights and trying to make life difficult for Agnes.

But those teenage summers in the South of France had, she realised in hindsight, not been all bad. Using French all day and every day improved her native language immensely. Agnes and she always spoke French together but English was the main language in her daily life at school and with her friends. Oscar rarely had time to entertain her and whilst Theo was always pleased to see her, there were times when he was busy too and she was left to her own devices for an hour or two.

As she grew older she spent more time with Theo than she did with Oscar. It was Theo who introduced her to friends of his who had teenage children so that she quickly built up a circle of friends for the holidays. It was Theo too who taught her to play tennis, took her to the theatre, shrugged his shoulders when she questioned why Oscar wanted her there when he couldn't be bothered to spend a lot of time with her. 'It's just the way he is,' he'd said. 'And I expect he's got a lot on his mind. Business and – and other things.'

She'd never asked about the 'other things' she'd simply accepted that Oscar had his secrets. It wasn't until much later that Francine began to understand that his secrets always involved a woman.

Theo had always accompanied her back to the UK at the end of her holiday, saying it was his yearly treat to spend time in Devon with her and Agnes...

Francine came to with a start as the bathroom door slammed and she heard Zazz run up to the attic bedroom. She'd be glad when the meeting with the notaire was over and they could begin to do whatever it was they needed to do. Deciding if there was anything Agnes wanted to keep from the house would be next, not that there was likely to be anything. And she herself definitely didn't want a thing. Getting ready to put the house up for sale would be the next step. It would be a huge job clearing the place of Oscar's possessions, clothes, books, furniture and all the other personal things he'd collected over the years. And then of course there was his boat to be disposed of. Theo would know whom to approach over that. Briefly Francine wondered about the boat. Where was it currently? What sort of boat was it – a sailing dinghy, a motorboat, or possibly even a proper yacht?

Francine stood up and grabbed a towel. All these questions would start to be answered tomorrow, right now she needed a shower. Ten minutes later as she stood in front of the bedroom mirror drying her hair, she saw a text message on her mobile from Edwin. Rather than text him back she pressed the call button and gave a happy smile when he answered.

'How was the flight?' Edwin asked. 'How does it feel to be back down in Cannes?'

'The flight was fine. But everything feels peculiar to me right now. Not helped by staying in Oscar's house.'

'I assumed you'd stay at Theo's,' Edwin said, surprised.

'Zazz insisted she was staying up here and I couldn't let her be alone. Agnes is happy down with Theo so that is something at least.'

'How is Zazz?'

'Truly? I'm not sure. I'd hoped that once the angsty teenage years were over she'd start to communicate with us again but,' Francine paused, 'I'm sure there's something going on in her life that she doesn't want me, us, to know about. Since we left Bath she seems to have become a stranger.'

There was a short silence. 'Maybe a few days in Cannes together will bring you closer again.'

'Hope so,' Francine said. 'We've got the notaire's meeting soon, after that we should be able to start working out what we can do this visit. I think we're going to have to come back a couple of times to sort things, empty the house out for a start, before we can get rid of the place.'

'Once you've seen the notaire you'll have an idea of all the necessary formalities and be able to work out a timescale. We can come over together later and organise things. Get a house clearance company in if necessary.'

'That's true. We don't have to do it all ourselves.'

'What are you all doing this evening?'

'Supper in a local restaurant and hopefully an early night.'

'Enjoy that then. I'll ring you in the morning.'

When Francine went downstairs ready to leave for the restaurant sometime later, Zazz was in the sitting room curled up on the sofa typing a WhatsApp message on her phone.

'Ready?' Francine asked, disconcertingly noting how completely at home Zazz looked sitting there.

'Two seconds,' Zazz said. 'Need to send this to a friend.' She pressed send and stood up. 'Let's go.'

'I think rue Saint Antoine is in this direction,' Francine said, locking the front door behind them and pointing to her left.

'It definitely is,' Zazz said, followed by 'What?' as Francine turned and looked at her.

'How could you possibly know that?'

'My friend Mr Google told me.' Zazz laughed lightly before quickly stepping in front of her mother to bypass another pedestrian. Rue Saint Antoine with its numerous restaurants, boutiques and jewellers was popular with locals as well as holidaymakers and its narrowness coupled with the crowds made it impossible to walk side by side. Talking to Zazz as she'd hoped to do as they walked was not going to happen, Francine realised, so she resorted to window shopping at several of the boutiques they passed. Zazz, a couple of metres in front of her, came back to join her as she stood for a moment in front of an upmarket boutique shop window filled with jewellery.

'What's caught your eye?' Zazz asked.

Francine pointed at a simple silver necklace with several small diamonds spaced around the chain. 'It's beautiful but gosh, the price tag!'

'I'll tell Dad you'd like it for Christmas, shall I?' Zazz said as they both moved away from the window. Francine laughed and shook her head.

'No point. It's way out of our Christmas present price range.'

13

Theo and Agnes were already seated at a table in the restaurant when they arrived and Theo stood up to greet them as the maître d' ushered them in.

Once they were seated and settled, a waiter placed a plate of hors d'oeuvres on the table whilst another lifted the bottle of champagne from its ice bucket and poured them each a glass.

Francine raised an eyebrow. 'Champagne?'

'I wanted to celebrate having you all together back in Le Suquet,' Theo said quietly. 'So the toast is, to the future.'

Raising their glasses they murmured, 'To the future.'

Zazz, conscious of Theo regarding her, his eyes with a definite questioning look, decided that this moment would be as good a time as any to tell her mother and grandmother what she had done. She took a few long sips of her drink for courage before looking at her mother.

'Mum, Granny, what I'm about to tell you is probably going to upset you but as Uncle Theo has pointed out to me, it would be more upsetting if I kept it secret and didn't tell you.'

Francine gave her a sharp look. 'I knew there was something on your mind.'

Zazz gave her a half smile. 'Mother's prerogative I guess,' she said before taking another sip of champagne. 'About a year ago I came to Le Suquet and introduced myself to my grandfather.'

Francine was the first to break the silence that descended after her words. 'You came here on your own to meet Oscar?'

Zazz nodded.

'Did you just turn up without warning?'

'Yes. Oscar was happy to finally meet me, we got on, and I liked him.' Zazz looked at her mother and grandmother defiantly.

'Why didn't you tell us before?' Francine said.

'Because I knew what your reaction was likely to be.'

'If he hadn't died, did you plan on keeping in contact? Make regular visits to see him?' Agnes asked quietly. 'Or was it a one-off visit to satisfy your curiosity?'

'I've been over a couple of times and,' Zazz hesitated, 'and I planned on further, longer visits.' Judging from their reactions now was not the time to admit she'd already been over a total of three times. As for her master plan, now was definitely not the moment to tell her mother about that. Inwardly she prayed that Theo would stay silent about that for now too.

Agnes turned to Theo. 'You knew about these visits, didn't you?' Theo gave her a brief nod.

'Why didn't you say something?'

'Zazz thought she should be the one to tell you and I agreed. She promised me she would – when the time was right.'

'My meeting with Oscar doesn't make any difference to you now anyway. He's dead.' Zazz finished her champagne and placed the glass on the table.

'You should have told us. I can't understand why you found it necessary to be so unbelievably deceitful,' Francine said.

'I'm sorry. But I knew you both would disagree with me meeting him and would try to stop me. As far as both of you are concerned, you'd fallen out with Oscar and therefore I couldn't have any contact either. But you've never explained why or what had happened in the past. You would never bring me to meet my grandfather so I took matters into my own hands. I'm glad I did before it was too late. But I'm sorry it's upset you.'

'Did Oscar explain his version of events to you?' Agnes asked quietly.

The waiter arrived at that instant, handing them menus and clearing the debris of aperitifs away. Zazz focused her attention on the menu, glad that the moment to answer her grandmother had been pushed aside.

Once they'd all chosen and given their orders to the waiter who collected the menus and departed, an uneasy silence descended around the table. Zazz bit her lip thoughtfully. Was it the right time to tell them about her plans for the future? Probably best to leave it for now. She could tell how hurt they were by her first announcement, goodness only knows how they would react to her real news.

Francine looked at Zazz thoughtfully. 'So that's why Cerise was all over you earlier – she clearly remembered you.'

'Probably.' Zazz turned to Theo. 'I've forgotten when the notaire's meeting is.'

'Tomorrow afternoon at two o'clock,' Theo said. 'I was thinking that perhaps I go to collect Oscar's ashes in the morning. If you like to come with me?' he asked, glancing around. 'Non? *D'accord* I collect alone but we need to decide what to do with him when I have him.'

The evening failed to recover from the bewilderment of Zazz's announcement, despite the good food and the wine that accompanied it. Theo did his best to lighten the atmosphere with some stories of events in Cannes that he and his friends had attended recently. A play in the Palais des Festivals, an art exhibition in one of the grand hotels on the Croisette and a vintage car display.

'I hope we can fit in some outings whilst you are all here,' he said. 'Make some new happy memories for you.'

But both Agnes and Francine struggled to respond with genuine enthusiasm. Zazz, uncomfortably aware that she was responsible for spoiling the evening, decided she was better off keeping quiet in case she added even more to the unhappy atmosphere that now existed between Francine, Agnes and herself.

Nobody appeared to want to linger after their meal was eaten and once Theo had paid the bill they made their way outside. After making an arrangement to meet up in the morning to explore Cannes a little and to maybe have lunch they said good-night. Francine and Zazz set off to walk silently back up to higher Le Suquet whilst Theo and Agnes turned in the opposite direction and went down towards the old harbour.

Once they were back in Oscar's house Zazz waited while Francine locked the front door before leaning in and kissing her on the cheek.

'Night, Mum. I've got a couple of e-mails to answer so I think I'll go straight up. I'm planning on going for a run in the morning – I'll pick up some croissants on my way back for breakfast so I'll see you then,' and before Francine could say anything, Zazz was running up the stairs to the attic.

'Goodnight,' Francine echoed. Obviously no mother – daughter chat happening tonight then, but had she really expected one?

14

The crowds on the street had thinned somewhat as they left the restaurant and when Theo tucked Agnes's arm under his own she didn't object and they were able to walk as a couple down towards the old harbour without being jostled. It was still light and as they waited to cross the road by the Gare du Bus Theo saw that Agnes was staring at the mural on the bus station wall.

'*Incroyable*,' she said, looking at the numerous *trompe l'œil* paintings depicting the history of cinema in Cannes.

'That painting celebrates one hundred years of cinema here in Cannes,' Theo said. 'Have you spotted Fred Astaire and Ginger Rogers yet? I know Jean-Paul Belmondo is there somewhere and Minnie Mouse too but I can't name all the names.'

'So beautiful. I can see Lauren Bacall,' Agnes answered, her gaze still fixed on the mural.

'You will see paintings like this all over Cannes,' Theo said. 'It all began after the millennium. We will go on a walk or two while you are here and I shall show the others to you. They all celebrate Cannes's great involvement with cinema.'

Once they'd crossed the street onto Quai Saint-Pierre they

strolled past the large pizza place and other restaurants that lined the road before making their way into the back lane that led to Theo's house.

'Will we have a nightcap together?' Theo asked. 'Or are you tired after the day and wish to go to bed?'

'I'd love a small drink,' Agnes said.

'*Bien*. I have some Saint Honorat liqueur I save for a special occasion. Tonight is that occasion. You go through to the yard, I fetch and we drink it under the stars.'

Sitting near the bougainvillea Agnes let her thoughts drift while she waited for Theo to reappear. Jasmine's confession this evening had been a surprise but Agnes recognised the truth in her words when she'd protested about being denied a meeting with her grandfather. She knew too, that she, more than Francine, had been guilty of ensuring the family split had passed down to the next generation by refusing to even acknowledge Oscar's existence from the day she arrived in England, forty-six years ago. Of course, she'd had to eventually accept Francine visiting him once a year. She was his daughter. No court would have tolerated her denying him access forever. But Jasmine was a different matter.

Agnes had seen no reason for them to ever meet and had persuaded Francine it was better that way. 'You don't want him filling the child's head with the kind of rubbish he tried to feed you with. He has no place in the next generation.' She could hear herself saying those words even now. Had she been right to lay the law down like that? She remembered Theo on one of his visits to see them, trying to persuade both of them to let bygones be bygones but that had been an impossible suggestion for her to even think about.

Dear Theo. A better friend than she truly deserved. She could never repay him for everything he had done for her and Francine.

Agnes sighed. It was too late now to make amends. If only. Theo appeared at that moment as if she'd conjured up his presence by thinking about him and she gave him what she hoped was a bright smile.

Theo handed her a small liqueur glass filled with a golden liquid. '*Santé.*' And they gently clinked glasses together.

'This is a day I despaired of ever seeing,' he said quietly. 'So many times I sit out here and wish you were here too. And finally, you are.'

'*Oui*, here I am,' Agnes said and gave a little nod of agreement. 'I do wish you'd told me that Jasmine had visited Oscar.'

'I couldn't do that without breaking my promise to Zazz. Besides, it was done. You still call her Jasmine? Zazz suits her better.' When Agnes looked at him but didn't reply he took a sip of his drink.

'Oscar changed a little in the last year,' Theo said quietly as though he was wary of her reaction to the mention of his brother. 'Zazz coming into his life like she did had a big impact on him, maybe it was that. Oh, he was still irascible and difficult to like and get on with but there was definitely something different about him. Once or twice recently I caught a strange look on his face as he glared at me. It was as though he was about to tell me something and then changed his mind, giving me a weird look and smiling. It was beginning to freak me out to be honest.' He gave Agnes an uncertain look. 'I didn't know how to respond. His temper was still a bit fiery.'

'Are you sure it wasn't a put-on act? Trying to make you uneasy over something he was planning. He was a very good actor when he wanted to be,' Agnes paused. 'Whenever he was unexpectedly nice to me I knew there would be a price to pay.'

'Je *suis très désolé, ma cherie,* that you suffered so much with him,' Theo said softly.

'All in the past, thankfully,' Agnes said. 'And largely due to your help.'

'I do wonder if perhaps, like the rest of us, the regrets over things done, or not done, began to mount up as the years passed.' Thoughtfully Theo took a sip of his drink. 'I know mine do.'

'I don't think anyone gets through life without regrets,' Agnes said quietly. 'I know I have more than a few too – some huge and some tiny but regrets all the same. Some people are incapable of recognising their own faults and I believe Oscar is, was, one of those. I don't believe he ever uttered the word *sorry* in his life. He certainly didn't to me.' Agnes stood up. 'I think I'm ready to go to bed. It's been a long day.'

'You discuss the notaire's meeting with Francine and Jasmine?' Theo asked as he too stood up. 'Perhaps give them a little warning of the possible problem?'

Agnes shook her head. 'No. I think we can both make a guess at what particular complication the notaire has discovered concerning the will – and that information will be better coming from him.'

Theo moved to her side. 'The rendez-vous with the notaire is going to be difficult but you know I will do anything to help you, Francine and Zazz to cope with whatever it is the notaire discloses.' He leant in and gently kissed her cheek. '*Bonne nuit, ma cherie,* sleep well.'

15

———

Zazz let herself out of the house as silently as she could the next morning and took the turning for rue Saint Antoine. Such a different street in the early morning to the one they'd walked last night. Few pedestrians and only the occasional cafe owner setting out the pavement tables and chairs ready for breakfast customers to avoid as she ran down. Once she was at the bottom she crossed the main road and took a quick picture of the boats in the old harbour.

Rufus had replied to her text from yesterday telling him she'd arrived with a simple thumbs up. Maybe a picture of the harbour and telling him about her new friend, Mel, whom she was meeting in about five minutes to go running with, would show him she hoped they could still be friends and maybe prompt him to send a proper reply? As she pressed the button to send the WhatsApp message Mel appeared alongside her.

She and Mel had met on her last but one visit to see Oscar and had become instant friends. Mel, only about six months older than her, had started her own holiday business a couple of summers ago, managing villas and apartments along the coast between Cannes and Cagnes-sur-mer. Intrigued when she heard about Zazz's lifestyle blog and the huge number of followers she had on various social media platforms, Mel had been her champion ever since. When Zazz had told her how much she longed to move over she'd said, 'Go for it. It's the perfect job for down here. The Riviera loves its social media influencers.' After Oscar's death, Zazz had e-mailed Mel about how her plans for spending the summer on the Riviera were now up in the air but she was still coming down and hoping to sort something out when she arrived.

'*Bonjour* Zazz. You made it. Let's make for the Quai Laubeuf.' Mel smiled at her and together they ran along the narrow pathway of Quai Saint Pierre, Running steadily they passed moored boats and went on towards the Quai Laubeuf where the tourist carrying boats for excursions to the Îles de Lérins were moored.

They stopped in the large car park attached to the *quai* and did some stretching exercises for a few moments. Out in the Bay of Cannes, the islands of Saint Marguerite and Saint Honorat were both bathed in the early morning sunlight. Zazz gave a happy sigh. 'I can't believe that I'm actually here,' she said.

'How are things with your maman?' Mel asked. 'You have told her your plans now?'

Zazz shook her head. 'I've told them about visiting Oscar but not my plans for this summer yet. I seriously think they will both freak out when I tell them. Maybe even disown me. I don't know.'

'I've told you there's always a bed for you at my place,' Mel said. 'It's not a problem, I promise.'

'Thank you. What are you up to today?'

'I've got to check out a villa in Juan-les-Pins, make sure it's ready for the guests I'm picking up from the airport this afternoon. In between I have to do some paperwork, do some Instagram promo and organise some dinner reservations for later in the week.' Mel smiled. 'It's all good. What about you?'

'I thought I'd pick up some tourist brochures, see if I could do a bit more in-depth research on places that looked promising and write a "Changing my lifestyle" piece for the blog. I've been teasing my followers now for weeks. Kickstart my new life like I'd planned.' Zazz glanced at her watch. 'I promised to pick up some breakfast croissants so I'd better start back.'

'Come on then, we'll run back together,' Mel said. 'Fancy joining me for a pizza this evening? Seven o'clock by the harbour?'

'I'll be there.'

* * *

Sleep had evaded Francine for most of the night. She finally dropped off at around four o'clock but was awake again at six when she heard Zazz creeping downstairs and letting herself out for her run. Francine sighed. Her daughter was so... prickly was the only word she could think of to describe her at the moment. Something was clearly going on in her life that she didn't want to talk about.

Francine pushed the duvet back and got up. Little point in staying in bed. She pulled on her jeans and a shirt, while Zazz was out she'd have a wander around the house. Banish some of the ghosts whilst she was on her own if she could. She'd start at the top and make her way down.

Climbing the spiral staircase into the attic she remembered the last time she'd climbed them thirty-six years ago...

The attic has been newly converted into a room just for you,' Oscar had said, smiling as he'd led the way up. An early present for her eighteenth birthday still a couple of months away. 'Somewhere you and your friends can hang out, play your pop music. No smoking though,' and he'd wagged his finger at her. The teenager in her had been thrilled. Until she'd learnt the conditions attached to the room. It wasn't to be used just for her summer visits. No. She had to come and live in Le Suquet full time.

Her first reaction had been to burst out with 'But I can't leave Maman on her own.'

Oscar's face had darkened. 'Of course you can. You will be an adult soon. You come and live with me, go to college here in France and want for nothing. It's your birthright. That's the deal anyway. Until you decide, you can stay in your old room. Your choice.' And he'd slammed the door shut before almost pushing her onto the new spiral staircase, forcing her to descend in front of him.

That incident had not only set the tone for the last week of her holiday but had shattered the tenuous relationship that had struggled to exist between her and Oscar.

Theo, when she tentatively asked his advice as to what she should do, had regarded her sadly. 'I'm désolé your father has put you in this difficult position. Whatever you decide is either going to hurt you, your mother or infuriate Oscar. But the truth is, you need to do what is best for you. This could turn out to be one of the major decisions of your life. And you need to be certain you are making the right one for you. I'm sure you will make the right choice. Please don't let him bully you.'

Francine avoided Oscar as much as she could for the next few days whilst she tried to work out what she should do. The pros and cons were written out and cross-checked time and time again. Sitting on the new bed up in the attic room she dreamt of the life she could lead if she took Oscar up on his offer. The thought of living on the Riviera was exciting and cool. Another part of her that loved living in Dartmouth couldn't help but acknowledge how different – even better? – her life could be in France. Her holidays in the South of France had given her a certain cache too amongst her friends. Moving here permanently would certainly raise that a notch. She longed to talk to her mum about it but Agnes was the one person she couldn't turn to for advice. There was only three days of her holiday left when Oscar unexpectedly appeared as she was making toast and coffee for her breakfast and impatiently demanded her answer.

'Decided yet?'

Francine shook her head. 'I don't know what to do. Living here, going to college, sounds a lovely idea and I'm seriously tempted but I keep thinking about Mum being on her own.' Her voice trailed away as Oscar looked at her, exasperated, before moving up close and staring intently at her. She shrank back but he leant in even closer.

'I'll help you decide then, shall I? I've got to go to San Remo for a business meeting, won't be back until tomorrow mid-day. If you are still here when I get back I shall take that as the sign you are staying to enjoy the life I am offering you. And I shall telephone your mother to tell her you're not returning to her. If you decide not to stay, I want you out of this house before I return. You can go back to your sad little life and your pathetic mother in England and regret the decision for the rest of your life. Got it?' As he spat out the last two words his hand shot out and swiftly gave her a blow on both cheeks.

It was the words 'sad little life and your pathetic mother' that blazed fire into Francine's brain more than her stinging cheeks. She didn't have a sad little life and Agnes was anything but pathetic. As she stared at Oscar she suddenly saw him for what he was. A man who presented a cultivated image to the world, at odds to the man he was behind closed doors. A man who dressed immaculately – this morning he was wearing a fashionable lightweight beige safari suit and carrying a leather briefcase – but strip away the expensive clothes and gold Cartier watch, he was nothing but a mean-spirited thug of a man. A man who thought he could coerce her to live her life on his terms.

'Got it,' she said, nodding as she stared him down, ignoring the pain *of her throbbing cheeks. 'If that's the way you treated my maman no wonder she left you. I'll leave this morning.'*

Oscar glared at her before turning and storming out of the kitchen. Francine screamed after him.

'And my maman is not pathetic. God knows what she ever saw in you. You're nothing compared to her and I HATE you. You are a despicable man.'

A door being slammed shut had been her only reply. Appetite gone, she'd binned the toast and threw the coffee down the sink. A quick shower before she packed her things, a cold flannel on her cheeks to calm them down, and she dragged her suitcase out onto the landing. Slowly she went up the spiral staircase to take one last look at the room that could have been hers only to find it locked.

Theo, when she arrived on his doorstep ten minutes later, took one look at her tear-stained face and pulled her in to give her a tight hug. The next day he changed their tickets and they drove to the airport. Her childhood was over.

16

Francine looked around the present-day attic room and wondered what Oscar had done with all the white modern Swedish furniture he'd chosen to try and bribe her with all those years ago. Zazz's belongings were spread out over the few good quality practical pieces that were now in the room. Francine took in the laptop, the notebooks and files, the camera and its tripod. The curtains on the alcove wardrobe were open and Zazz's clothes were hung crammed together on the rail, underwear and a hoody were on the shelves alongside.

Smiling to herself, Francine went back downstairs. Zazz clearly took after her. Edwin always teased her about the size of her suitcase whenever they went away. She always overpacked, worried that she'd need another top, an extra cardigan or even a strapless bra to wear under the off-the-shoulder blouse that she'd thrown into the suitcase at the last moment. The art of minimalistic packing was clearly not in their family genes.

On the first-floor landing, Francine moved on past the bathroom before stopping in front of the door of the bedroom her parents had shared, her hand on the white porcelain doorknob.

The memories she had of this room were almost sepia-coloured in her mind, belonging as they did to her early childhood, before Agnes had run away with her to England. Happy memories in the main, involving her and Agnes reading or sipping hot chocolate, snuggled up together in the big bed when Oscar was out. Events that Francine knew had to be kept secret from her father. He would have considered Agnes to be spoiling her. Very few of her memories of this time featured Oscar. He'd been a bystander in her early childhood, never an active participant, despite Agnes urging him to relax and simply play childish games with her.

When she'd visited as a teenager she'd instinctively realised this particular room would always be strictly off limits to her, although Oscar had never indicated that in so many words. The one time she'd peeped inside the room, all the feminine accessories, like the *toile de jouy* curtains and matching bedspread her mother had decorated the space with, had disappeared. Instead, it had been turned into a stark masculine room, with grey walls and dark bed linen.

Francine tightened her grip on the doorknob and slowly turned it, pushing the door open, unsure as to what she'd find.

The big bed was unmade, a crystal chandelier hanging over it cloudy with grime, the dressing table dusty. An air of abandonment and neglect hung over everything. Francine pulled the door closed again and turned away. Where had Oscar slept in recent years? There was only one room left.

Curious, Francine opened the door of her childhood bedroom, the one she'd suggested Zazz slept in. To her surprise, this room with its no-nonsense furnishings, pale blue walls and cream scatter rugs on the terracotta tiles appeared to have been Oscar's bedroom. The bedclothes were roughly pushed back as if Oscar had just got up, pyjamas left in a heap on top of the duvet, a towel untidily placed on the rail, a discarded shirt flung over the back of the cane bedroom chair. An old-fashioned four-drawer bureau stood in front of the window, a French vanity mirror placed on its top. Francine remembered helping Agnes to clean the dressing-table mirror and polish its fancy wooden frame with its two shallow drawers when it had been in the old bedroom. On the bureau top was also a comb and a pair of nail clippers. One of its drawers was open, filled with neatly folded socks. Francine turned away.

Back down in the kitchen Francine put the kettle on, found a teapot and tea bags and stared out of the window, her thoughts, like the water in the kettle about to boil, bubbling away, untamed. The house needed to be cleared. What were they going to do with everything? How would Agnes react to being back in the house? How long had Zazz stayed with Oscar for? Had Theo started the process of contacting people to tell them about Oscar? What to do with the ashes once he'd collected them? How long would they have to stay in Le Suquet? And why did the prospect of a long stay fill her with anxiety? Oscar was dead. He was incapable of hurting them any more.

17

Theo had left to collect Oscar's ashes and Agnes was washing the breakfast cups and plates when Francine and Zazz arrived at the cottage.

'Has Theo taken Cerise?' Zazz asked, disappointed there was no sign of the little dog.

'Yes. She adores the car. Do we have a plan for this morning?' Agnes asked.

'Just have a wander I thought,' Francine said. 'See how much has changed. Shall we start with Marché Forville? That should still be much the same. Maybe we can pick up a few things for lunch or supper tonight.'

The large covered market was bustling just as Agnes and Francine remembered it although they both admitted they'd forgotten how many stalls there were: vegetables, cheese, cooked and fresh meat, olive oil, herbs, socca, soaps, lavender, cream, eggs, soft fruits and flowers. After a quick conference Francine bought some cheese, fresh cream, eggs and some green salad leaves. 'That's lunch sorted. Cheese omelette and *salade*.'

Leaving the market by the lower entrance they wandered

down towards the harbour. Francine and Agnes marvelling with each other at how busy the place had become but changed so little. Passing the Hôtel du Ville Agnes stopped and stared around. Something she tried not to ever do if she were honest, was to think about her marriage. But standing there in front of the imposing nineteenth-century four-storey building, it was inevitable. Watching the French national flag over the porch-like entrance to the building fluttering in the on-shore breeze off the Mediterranean, the memory of the time that her life had changed irrevocably for the worse fell unwanted into her consciousness...

The foggy daze that had enveloped her whole being as Oscar had pushed the diamond ring onto her finger had rarely lifted in the few weeks leading to the wedding day. Through her parents discussing wedding arrangements, through choosing a dress to be married in, through cake tasting and through ensuring her passport was up to date, through it all, she sleepwalked. It might be the 1960s as she'd once told Oscar but the changes of the decade were conspicuous by their absence in her own life. Plans to escape drifted in and out of her consciousness: where to go; how to survive; would she get a job easily; would her parents miss her – be angry? Disown her? Theo would help her to run away but could she actually do it?

At one point she even thought of trying to find her sister, Denice, and asking for her advice. But that was something else she didn't know how to go about. Nobody had heard from Denice for a couple of years; she could be anywhere in the world. She could have changed her name, anxious to put the past behind her.

Even after her papa had told him it was impossible to stop the wedding and told him to leave her alone, Theo continued to beg her to stand up to both her parents and Oscar and say NO. Ever since that morning when he'd turned up with a black eye he'd been pleading with her to run away with him. Telling her how much he loved her and would take care of her.

Four nights before the wedding, Oscar had gone to Monaco with some friends for 'my last weekend of freedom', as he'd joked to Agnes, who'd known he didn't mean a word of it. She knew he was a ladies' man, as Theo had politely put it and knew that was unlikely to change once they were married. Theo had been given a 'come if you want to but I don't care if you don't' invitation by Oscar for the Monaco weekend but refused point-blank to go. Instead, he'd persuaded Agnes to spend time with him that Saturday afternoon in Antibes where they could have a final dinner together. If truth were told, Agnes hadn't taken much persuading. Her feelings for Theo ruled her heart in those last days before the wedding. If she was marrying Theo she would have been the happiest girl alive.

Antibes, the afternoon they spent there, was wonderful. Hand in hand the two of them walked the ramparts, enjoyed a glacé and strolled through the narrow streets of the old town. In one of the hidden away streets Theo took her into a jewellers' where he bought her a silver Celtic Knot pendant which he placed lovingly around her neck. And finally they wandered around the harbour where the private yachts were moored. Both conscious all the time that they were making memories that had to last them a lifetime. Theo had told her earlier as they strolled through the old town that he was leaving on the morning of the wedding. The band had been contracted for a tour of Europe. He would be away for months.

Just as Agnes was beginning to feel hungry and wonder where they were to have dinner, Theo stopped by a shiny well maintained motor yacht with a large notice tied to its guardrails reading 'Available for Hire' and called out a greeting. Instantly a man appeared on the aft deck.

'Monsieur Bois. Everything is ready for you and your wife. The caterers have delivered your meal. Champagne is in the fridge. Any problems, I'm on the third yacht in that direction,' and he pointed to his right. 'Your Cinderella hour is ten o'clock. Enjoy your evening.' And he leapt off the boat onto the quay.

'You've hired the yacht for the evening?' Agnes said, deciding not to question the way the man had thought her to be Theo's wife. She'd pretend and cherish the impossible idea of it being true for the evening.

'For the next three hours anyway. I thought we'd have more privacy than eating in a restaurant. We both know Oscar has his spies everywhere.'

'Was that the reason for the ridiculous Bois nom de plume?' Agnes said laughing. Theo nodded.

Agnes started exploring. A galley, a salon with white leather furniture and scarlet velvet cushions, a bathroom with a large shower, and marble and gold decorations everywhere. Agnes gasped at the sight of it. She'd never seen such an over-the-top bathroom. A narrow gangway with two small cabins on either side, lead to the master cabin at the front of the yacht. Theo was fiddling with the stereo system as she wandered back through to the salon where an open bottle of champagne and two glasses now stood on the table. Slotting a tape into the machine, Theo pressed a button and as music began to play Agnes whispered, 'I wish you weren't leaving.'

'Change your mind and come with me? Please.' Theo begged, turning to her.

'I can't.' She couldn't tell him how much she longed to run away with him and turned away, biting her lip.

Gently he pulled her towards him and took her in his arms before bending his head and kissing her. Responding to his kiss, Agnes leant into his body and knew that she was powerless to stop whatever followed. And didn't want to.

Sometime later, laying there in Theo's arms fingering the necklace and listening to the emotional words of 'The Windmills of Your Mind' drifting in the air, Agnes wiped a tear away. A tear of happiness. A tear for what might have been. A tear for what would never be.

And never again would she hear 'The Windmills of Your Mind' without crying and remembering the most wonderful evening of her life.

Two mornings later there had been no sign of Theo as she arrived at the Cannes Hôtel de Ville. True to his word, he'd gone. It was in that instant that Agnes knew if he'd been there and held out his hand, she would have taken it and run away with him whatever the consequences of her action. She knew her life without him was going to be a sad one.

Even as she walked into the room on her father's arm, clutching her bouquet to her body like a shield, and allowing him to leave her at a smiling Oscar's side, she was still inwardly questioning herself about what on earth was she doing. She shouldn't be doing this. She loved Theo, not Oscar. Her mouth opened but no words came. It wasn't until the mayor finished his introductory speech to the legal ceremony that she finally acknowledged to herself she'd left it way too late to do anything to stop her inevitable marriage to Oscar. She wasn't brave enough to say no in the middle of the ceremony, not with her parents standing at her side in the wooden panelled room with its decorative ceiling, where the brief ceremony was held. It would humiliate them as well as Oscar. She couldn't do it to them. And who knew how Oscar would react? What revenge he would exact?

She'd zoned out of the rest of the legal formalities, knowing when she left the room she would be a different person. Mrs Agnes Agistini. Whoever that would turn out to be.

Sadly, the old cliché 'life's a bitch' had turned out to be only too true for Agnes Agistini née Bernard…

Agnes swallowed hard. In the words of another popular song of that time, 'Like a Puppet on a String', she'd allowed herself to be used by both her parents and Oscar. He'd wanted a wife he could control to show his respectability as a married man to the world. And her parents, her father in particular, had wanted her married before she came of age and whilst he still had the last word on what she did. What a naive wimp she'd been to go along with what was virtually an arranged marriage. Her relationship with her parents had never recovered from what Agnes regarded as their betrayal. If only she'd been brave enough to run away with Theo her whole life would have been so different.

'Maman, are you okay?' Francine asked, gently touching Agnes's arm.

The touch pulled Agnes back into the present moment and she nodded. 'Shall we have the coffee we promised ourselves?' she said turning away from the Hôtel de Ville.

'There's a lovely cafe just along here,' Zazz said pointing across the road.

'Your friend Mr Google showed you that, I presume?' Francine said.

Zazz shook her head impatiently. 'No. Oscar gave me the grand tour when I came.'

She turned to her mother. 'I'm sorry that came out the way it did, but honestly I can't keep pretending that I've never been here before.'

'Being honest didn't bother you before,' Francine snapped.

'Please stop,' Agnes said, looking from one to the other. 'There is very little point in us falling out over something that can't be changed. You shouldn't have sneaked down here the way you did.' She gave Zazz a hard look. 'But you and I, Francine, have to accept it and move on.' Agnes took a deep breath. 'It is hard to believe he is gone and has no place in our lives any more but Oscar is dead. Let's go to the cafe and have an apricot croissant with our coffee.'

The cafe felt strangely familiar to Francine. Once they were settled at a table inside, as the tables on the pavement were all occupied, she looked around. Three decades ago the decor had been left over from the seventies with a grumpy owner behind the counter who had little time for his teenage customers. Today it was ultra-modern and bright with modern art on the walls and comfortable rattan chairs. The barista busy working the large coffee machine seemed vaguely familiar to Francine – a grown-up version of someone she'd known in the past when he caught her glance but he didn't so much as look at her again, he was so busy.

Sipping her coffee, Francine started to wonder if any of her old friends were still around and a rueful smile crossed her face. Thirty-six years since she'd left so it was highly unlikely that they would recognise her – or she them for that matter – even if there was anyone from her past still living in Cannes. But she couldn't help giving the middle-aged barista a second glance and wondering.

Agnes confessed to feeling a little tired as they drank their coffee and ate the delicious coffee eclairs they'd decided on instead of apricot croissants. 'I think I've done enough sight-seeing for our first day.'

'Are you okay?' Francine gave her an anxious glance.

'I'm fine but a rest before this afternoon's meeting would be good.'

Walking back to the cottage they met up with Theo and Cerise who instantly made a beeline for Zazz. Laughing, she took the lead from Theo and walked her the rest of the way. Whilst Agnes went for a rest the others turned the purchases from the market into lunch.

'I hope Maman is well,' Francine said, grating the cheese for the omelettes. 'I hope this trip is not too much for her.'

Theo looked at her. 'I think the memories it is stirring up are very hard for her. We must make sure she does not get melancholic.'

18

The notaire's office located in a street off the Croisette had an old-fashioned serious air about it. Shown into a meeting room, the four of them shook hands with Monsieur Caumont, the notaire, who was waiting for them before taking their places around the long highly polished oak table and sitting on matching chairs with green leather padded seats. The notaire sat on the large carver chair at the head of the table, a thick folder of papers in front of him.

He looked at Agnes. 'As his wife you—'

'Ex wife,' Francine interrupted. 'They were divorced years ago.'

'*Non.* I do not think so,' the notaire answered. 'I have been the deceased's notaire now for many years, I would know about the divorce. And Monsieur Agistini refers to her as his wife in his most recent will, dated six months ago. I have a copy of the will here for you,' and he passed a large envelope down the table to Agnes.

Wide-eyed, Francine looked at her mother. 'We were still

married,' Agnes said quietly. Francine closed her eyes and shook her head in disbelief.

'To continue,' the notaire said. 'Agnes, as his wife, inherits the right to live in the house until her death, or if she agrees to move out, a quarter of the value of the whole estate. You, Francine, as his only child, inherit the rest. There is also a small gift of five thousand euros for Jasmine Mansell. Straightforward French inheritance rules apply. But.' He paused. 'The reason I ask you to come is not because the will itself is complicated as it stands. The complication I need to talk to you about is that someone has come forward claiming to be Oscar's son and as such has a claim on his estate. Should it prove to be a true claim, it changes how the will would need to be applied.'

'As a male will he have a greater claim on the estate than anyone else? Like Maman?' Francine asked.

'Not a greater claim but a shared one. All children, legitimate or illegitimate, have an equal claim. In this case it means the two of you would share the residue of the estate, after Madame Agistini's quarter share.'

Silence greeted his words. It was Agnes who broke the silence. 'Do we know this man's name?'

'Serge Cortez.'

'Wouldn't he use the name Agistini if he was Oscar's son?' Zazz asked.

'His mother chose not to name his father on the birth certificate – another *petit complication* – so it is his mother's married name he uses. As does his own son.'

'How old is this Serge Cortez?' Agnes asked quietly.

'Fifty-one.'

Agnes gave a thoughtful nod at his reply.

'His maman accompanied him to see me and has signed an affidavit swearing that Oscar was the father of her son. However,' the notaire paused, 'I would be failing in my legal duty if I didn't advise you to apply to the court for permission to have a DNA test done to confirm. And I have told him this. Unfortunately, he is not happy about it, although he knows he has little choice if he wants to follow through with his claim.'

'Maybe he and his mother are lying then?' Francine said.

'I did explain very carefully to Madame Cortez the legal penalties for lying in this instance and she assured me she was letting the truth be known now for her son. And he has now agreed to having one done but there is a condition attached.'

'What is the condition?' Theo asked.

'That Francine proves she is Oscar's daughter by having a DNA test too.'

'That's ridiculous. My parents were married at the time of my birth,' Francine said crossly. 'Of course he was my father. Anyway, surely it's impossible to do a DNA test – I understand you need saliva or something like a strand of hair and Oscar is dead and already cremated.'

'It is still possible to do a paternal DNA test,' the notaire said. 'It would involve both mothers as well as you and Serge. If the house hasn't been cleared or cleaned it might be an idea to look in Oscar's bedroom. There may possibly be a comb with some strands of his hair caught in the teeth,' he shrugged. 'It would be worth you taking a look to make things easier.'

Francine sighed. '*D'accord*. But surely we can do a DNA paternity test ourselves – we don't need to involve the court. That is bound to hold things up.'

Monsieur Caumont shook his head. 'Personal DNA tests are illegal here in France. The only way to do them is with official permission that is granted through the court.'

'What happens if we simply accept the fact that he is Oscar's son as his mother has sworn on oath that he is and proceed on that basis?' Agnes asked quietly.

The notaire gave her a serious look. 'You would do that?'

'Maman, you shouldn't just accept a stranger's word and give away our rights.'

'I agree with your daughter and would advise strongly against that action,' Monsieur Caumont said. 'Whilst the signed affidavit makes it highly probable that Serge Cortez is genuinely Oscar's illegitimate son, it should be fully investigated and proved and that, to my mind, means a paternal DNA test.'

Agnes sighed. 'I need to let this news sink in and think about what to do.'

Theo pushed his chair back and stood up. 'It's a lot to take in and we need to discuss it. Can we make a rendez-vous in a few days?'

The notaire started to pick up his folder and pulled out a sealed envelope before replacing the papers he'd taken out earlier. 'Certainly. Serge Cortez asked me to give you this at the end of our meeting,' and he held the envelope out to Agnes. 'He told me it is from his mother. If it makes a problem for you then I would ask you to let me know the contents. *D'accord*?'

'*Merci*,' Agnes said, nodding in agreement, and put it in her handbag together with the copy of the will the notaire had passed to her earlier.

'Let me show you out. I'll see you in a few days' time then, when hopefully you have reached the decision to allow me to instigate the DNA tests. *A bientôt*.'

19

Back at the house, and despite it only being three o'clock, Theo poured them each a large glass of wine and put bowls of crisps and cashew nuts on the table out in the courtyard.

Francine took a slow long drink of her rosé before turning to her mother. 'Honestly, I can't believe you were still married to Oscar. Why on earth didn't you divorce him?'

Agnes gave a small shrug. 'Well, I couldn't see myself getting married again, we lived in different countries and divorces are expensive so I figured there was very little point. And in the beginning I was also worried about Oscar being difficult over you.'

Zazz reached for a handful of crisps. 'But once Mum was married, you could have divorced him then.'

'I did raise the possibility a few years ago but Oscar was of the opinion that even a no-fault divorce after so many years of separation was unnecessary. We could just carry on as we were. The truth is I expect it suited Oscar to say he had a wife somewhere even if she never put in an appearance. Knowing how difficult he could be, how much paperwork would be generated between

French and English courts, I couldn't summon up the energy to fight him. Now I don't have to and I'm finally free.' Agnes smiled before taking a long drink of her wine.

'Well, whatever happens with this Serge man, you are at least going to finally get some money from Oscar as his widow,' Francine said. 'Whether you want it or not.'

'Talking of Serge, you haven't opened the envelope the notaire gave you,' Theo said quietly.

Agnes picked up her handbag from the side of her chair, took out the envelope and carefully opened it.

'Is it from his mother as he claimed it to be?' Francine said.

Agnes looked at the signature and nodded. 'Yes. It's signed Rachel Cortez.' Silently she read the short letter before looking up at them. 'It simply says she wants us, me, to meet her, to talk.' Agnes folded the letter and replaced it in the envelope.

'Are you going to meet her?' Francine said. 'I'm not sure it's a good idea – depends on what she wants or hopes to achieve. I'm coming with you if you decide to meet her.' She held up her hand as Agnes went to say something. 'That's non-negotiable.'

'I'll think about it,' Agnes said. 'We also need to meet Serge himself I think.'

It was Theo who broke the silence that developed after her words.

'The notaire didn't mention any other bequests,' he said thoughtfully. 'But I'm not sure what happens about clearing the house now. I suspect we need to wait until we learn the truth about Serge and that could take weeks, even months, to discover.'

'Do you think he is going to want anything – other than his share of the house of course when it sells? What happens if we decide not to sell it immediately? Can we do that? The two of us against him? We could come down for holidays. Use it as a second home. Spend winter down here in the sun. You could even move back down and live in it permanently, Maman, if you wanted,' Francine said.

'I have absolutely no intention of staying in, yet alone living in, that house ever again,' Agnes said. 'I personally want it on the market as soon as possible.'

'I can see things dragging on for weeks, in typical French fashion,' Francine said. 'I'm not sure about staying down here indefinitely. If we can't make a start on sorting out the house. maybe we should think about going home and come back down in a couple of weeks. Personally, I can't just sit around doing nothing.' She heaved a heavy sigh. 'Everything has got so complicated with this challenge to the will.'

'I'm not planning on leaving,' Zazz said. 'I don't have anything to rush back for.'

'What do you mean? You've got a job. Responsibilities. Rent to pay,' Francine said sharply.

Zazz shook her head and took a deep breath. 'Not any more. I've left my job, given up my flat share and had already planned on spending at least the next nine months to a year down here. If not longer.' A stunned silence greeted her words.

'How long have you been planning this for?' Francine finally found her voice and glared at her daughter. Could this day throw up any more surprises?

'Since the end of last year.'

'You didn't think to mention it before?'

'I was coming home to tell you my plans, talk it over with you, book my ticket and then Oscar died and everything changed. And don't worry, I'll pay you back for my ticket.'

'That's the least of my worries,' Francine said. 'What are you going to do down here? Where are you going to live? And what about money? It's expensive to live down here.'

Zazz smothered a sigh. 'Mum, I'm not a child any more, I do

know how to look after myself. I have organised things and I have savings. You know I've been blogging for a couple of years now, well, in the last year or so I've grown my followers on both the blog and other social media platforms that I've signed up to, including Instagram and YouTube. I need to keep up the momentum now and expand with some different interesting content.'

'You can't seriously expect to make enough money to live on from social media,' Francine said.

Zazz nodded. 'I do but if necessary, I'll get an extra part-time job over summer for some cash flow.'

'But where are you going live? Apartments, even studios, down here are silly prices to rent.'

There was a split-second pause before Zazz said, 'Oscar said I could stay with him for as long as I wanted. I'm hoping that you and Granny,' she flashed Agnes a smile, 'will keep to that arrangement – at least until you and now this new relative of ours, sell the house. If not, I'll find somewhere else.' She helped herself to a handful of cashews from the dish on the table. 'I'm meeting a friend later for a pizza, so I'm going to head back to the house now. See you later,' and she quickly turned and made her way through the cottage and out of the front door.

'We've barely been here twenty-four hours – how the hell has she made a friend so quickly?' Francine said, glancing first at Agnes who was biting her lip and then at Theo.

'It's out of the question her living in Oscar's old house on her own. And what the hell did she mean about an "extra" job?' Francine's shoulders slumped. What was going on with Zazz? And why had Agnes always let her believe she'd divorced Oscar years ago? How many more secrets were going to surface over the coming days?

20

Back at the house Zazz opened up her laptop and tried to concentrate on researching more about the vineyards on the island of Saint Honorat where the monks from the Abbey there made world-famous wines and liqueurs. The history of The Man in the Iron Mask on the other island, Saint Marguerite, was fascinating too. The little information she'd read about both of them in the tourist brochures she'd picked up had sparked a couple of ideas for longer features.

Her mind though, was still buzzing with thoughts about the meeting at the notaire's. An illegitimate son of Oscar had to be some sort of family relation. Granny Agnes would be his step-mother, her mother would be his half-sister – and she would be his niece. And Theo would have a nephew. An instant extended dysfunctional family. Having to share the house inheritance with a complete stranger was a bit of a blow for her gran and mum. She was grateful for the five thousand euros Oscar had left her though.

The other thing that kept breaking into her concentration was whether her mum and Granny Agnes would agree to her staying in the house for the next few weeks at least. They were clearly less than happy with her after hearing her plans. It was fine for Mel to tell her not to worry she could always stay at hers until she found somewhere but although it was a relief to have that as Plan B, she desperately wanted to stick to her own Plan A. If only to prove to her parents that she was capable of organising a life on her own terms.

A WhatsApp message pinged into her phone. Rufus. Another thumbs up gif acknowledging the morning photo of the boats with no message. Zazz glared at the phone. Okay, she got that she'd hurt him by not talking about her plans but not answering her messages with actual words was a bit mean. She pressed the button to call him, determined to try and smooth things over between them. But her call went straight to voice message. Leaving a message was pointless. She wanted to talk to him. But in the end she sent him a text.

> Lots of exciting things to tell you. Please ring me. x

A moment later a text pinged in.

> Got a new job. Leaving for the US in ten days.
> Have a good life.

Zazz starred at the text in disbelief for almost a minute, unable to believe what she was reading before she pressed his number with a shaking hand. She needed to talk to him.

The number had been blocked. The man who had accused her of shutting him out of her life, had actually said those very words, 'I'd never shut you out of my life like that' had done just that. Rufus had dumped her. At the time he'd been accusing her of deceit and shutting him out had he been planning to do the same to her in a week or so? Well, at least she knew where she was now. Rufus was in the past and she was in the South of France determined to make her new life a success.

* * *

After Zazz left, Francine washed the glasses before telling Agnes and Theo that she was going to go for a walk by the harbour and then would head back to Oscar's house. 'Need some sea breeze to clear my head.' She didn't add that she desperately needed some time alone to phone Edwin and try to make sense of everything.

'Shall we follow Zazz's lead and go for a pizza tonight?' Theo suggested.

'Good idea,' Francine said. 'See you back here about seven?'

Leaving Theo's, Francine walked slowly down to the old harbour and strolled along. The pungent smell of fish hung in the air as she passed two or three fishermen sitting on upturned lobster pots on the quay mending their nets. None of the boats moored alongside the quay were as big as the ones she was used to seeing in Dartmouth, with their large wheelhouses and big inboard engines. These wooden work boats, scarcely bigger than a large dinghy with either small inboard engines or just an outboard motor clamped to the stern, looked more suitable for an inshore lake than the Mediterranean Sea to Francine. Briefly, she wondered how on earth with such small craft they managed to catch enough fish to earn a living.

Further along the quay she passed several small fibreglass yachts before slowing to admire a beautiful classic sailing boat, its varnished hull and stainless-steel deck fittings gleaming in the afternoon sun. A man busy coiling ropes on the port side of the yacht glanced in her direction and she recognised the man she'd seen in the cafe that morning. She definitely felt that she knew him. That he had been a part of her past. As she stared at him trying to work out who he was he smiled at her.

'I thought it was you this morning. Want to come on board, Frankie?'

She gave him a startled look. Nobody had called her Frankie for years and then there had only ever been one person who dared to.

'Piers?'

'The one and only.' He held out his hand to help her jump on board.

'I thought it was you this morning,' he said. 'But I was too busy to come over and check. You've still got that lovely smile of yours.'

'I'm surprised you recognised me,' Francine said. 'There was something familiar about you I couldn't quite place. And it was a different cafe.' She smiled at him. 'I've got it now though – it's your hair.' Piers's hair had always been the bane of his life but the envy of all her girlfriends. Thick and curly, his father had insisted he had a close crew cut which he hated. Now it had a fair amount of silver and grey amongst the black curls and whilst this morning it had been tied back in a man bun, now it was long and untamed. 'It really suits you.'

'Thank you, my papa, he still not like my hair. It's great to see you. I heard about Oscar. Is that why you're here?'

Francine nodded, glad that Piers hadn't offered his condolences. 'Yes. First time for thirty-six years and I have to say it feels more than weird being back.'

'Time for a coffee? Or a glass of wine?'

'A glass of wine would be lovely,' Francine said. 'It's been a bit of a day.'

'Grab a seat in the cockpit and I'll fetch us a bottle and some glasses and we can have a good catch-up.'

Francine sat in the cockpit as instructed and let her thoughts drift back to the days when she and Piers had been part of the group she'd hung around with for those two weeks of summer every year. That last holiday before her eighteenth birthday the gang had made the most of their soon-to-be curtailed freedom. University or full-time work loomed for everyone in a few weeks and they all knew that their lives would inevitably change direction. Days were spent swimming, sailing, picnicking under the stars on the beach, nighttime sails over to Saint Marguerite. The drastic change to her own life when Oscar had virtually thrown her out of the house had caught Francine unawares. She'd never expected to lose touch with her friends virtually overnight.

Piers climbed up into the cockpit and handed Francine a glass of wine. As they clinked glasses he said. '*Santé*. Here's to old friends.'

'Old friends,' Francine said, remembering how close the two of them had been that last summer. There had been no time to see anybody before she had flown home. Besides she'd been too upset to even try to say goodbye to anyone, especially Piers. She couldn't face telling him what had happened. If only she'd realised it would be so long before she saw him again.

Piers took a sip of his wine before looking at her. 'After you disappeared without saying goodbye I went to see Theo. He explained what had happened with Oscar and that he had no idea when or if you would be back. He advised me to be patient.'

'That sounds like Theo. Years too late to apologise but I'm sorry for running away like that. Not telling you I had to leave.'

'I was patient like Theo suggested. I'd hoped to hear from you before I went off to uni. But.' Piers gave her a rueful glance. 'Once there I became busy and involved and my life set off on the road to bring me to where I am today. Like they say, life is full of roads not travelled, isn't it?'

'Yes. Have you been happy?' Francine asked quietly. 'That is the main thing we can hope for. To be happy with the way life turns out despite everything we do to sabotage it.' As she spoke, she realised that Oscar with his continual striving for material things and his controlling nature had probably never been truly happy in himself for his whole life.

'Yes. I have a family and life is good.' Piers smiled. 'I hope you are too?'

'Yes. Current circumstances aside, I have a happy life,' Francine smiled. 'This is a beautiful boat. Is she yours? I remember you being sailing mad.'

Piers nodded. 'She's all mine. If you fancy a sail whilst you're here, just ask. You down here on your own?'

'Maman and my daughter are with me. You mentioned your family?'

'Two boys and a girl. Dominic, who works in the coffee shop with me now I've taken it over from Papa and Andre who works part-time in the cafe. My daughter, Armelle, is a bit of a free spirit but knows what she wants and is determined to get it, has started her own business. My wife ran off with a super-yacht owner a few years ago.'

'Sorry to hear that.'

Piers shrugged philosophically as he topped up their glasses. 'Mimi was always a fan of the bright lights and big spenders. I'm surprised she'd stayed with me for twenty years to be honest.'

'You married Mimi?' Francine couldn't keep the surprise out of her voice. 'I'd never have put the two of you together. I remember the two of you always sparring when we all hung out together.'

'Theo, he tell me you marry an Englishman several years ago?'

'Yes, Edwin. We have a daughter, Zazz – Jasmine really but

she hates that name, too old-fashioned for her.' Francine shrugged. 'What she calls herself is the least of my worries at the moment.'

Piers looked at her, waiting for her to continue. When she did continue it was to change the subject, not wanting to talk about her problems with Zazz.

Francine looked at Piers, puzzled. 'The cafe this morning? I don't remember it belonging to your family. I remember one near the market?'

'The position of the current one is much better business wise,' Piers said. 'One of the first things I did was to sell the old place and buy it.'

'How come you took over the family cafe? I remember you planned to go travelling after uni and then—'

'I was going to change the world,' Piers laughed. 'I did go travelling for six months and then reality hit. I was needed back here, so.' He drank some wine. 'I surprise myself how much I like working in the cafe, besides, I get to go sailing on this beauty several times a week.'

'Oscar had a boat, apparently. Do you know where he moored it? What it is like?' Francine asked looking around at the boats tied to the quay.

'It is berthed in the marina at Golfe-Juan. He was lucky the berth came with the boat, long waiting lists for moorings everywhere these days. It's a fifty-foot motorboat. I forget its name.'

'Quite a big one then. I must get Theo to check what's happening about it – if he knows.' Francine finished her wine. 'I'd better get back to the house. It's been great catching up a little.'

'I'm down here most evenings,' Piers said, standing up and taking her glass. 'Come and say hi anytime. I'm sure there's lots more to learn about each other's lives.'

'I might just do that,' Francine said. 'Escape from all the

family turmoil over Oscar's will.' She stood up and took Piers's offered hand to step up onto the stern of the yacht. 'I don't suppose you know a man called Serge Cortez, do you?'

Piers looked thoughtful. '*Non*. I don't think so. Is he important?'

Francine pulled a face. 'Who knows. But he could turn out to be my half-brother.'

'Knowing Oscar's reputation, I'm not surprised. Hope it's just the one. Sorry, Frankie,' he apologised as he registered the wince on Francine's face at his words.

She shook her head. 'Don't be. I hadn't even thought about there being more. I hope you're wrong for Maman's sake.' Francine stepped on to the quay and turned to face Piers. 'Thanks for the wine.'

'Ciao.'

Francine walked back up to Le Suquet deep in thought. Meeting Piers had opened a floodgate of memories and added in several new thoughts about Zazz's actions. Oscar's too. Had he been the one to put the idea of coming to live down here in Zazz's head? Or had Zazz had an ulterior motive when she first decided to secretly visit and meet her grandfather? However much Zazz said she was glad to have met him and how much they'd liked each other, Oscar would definitely have taken advantage of the situation. There had to be an ulterior motive for him to invite her to live down here. There was no way he would have done it out of the kindness of his heart. Francine gave a deep sigh. She knew exactly what his motive would have been. He'd wanted to be able to crow with satisfaction over his ability to entice his grand-daughter away from her mother and especially her grandmother.

But the biggest personal realisation of all came as she unlocked the front door of Oscar's house. Zazz had planned to do the very thing that she herself had been offered – the opportunity to stay with Oscar and live on the French Riviera. Her daughter had seized the chance that she herself had spent a large part of her life regretting turning down, whilst knowing at the same time, she'd done the only thing she could possibly do. There had never been a choice for her. After the sacrifices and the hardship that Agnes had suffered on her behalf, leaving her to live down here with Oscar had never truly been even a tiny possibility in her mind.

21

Agnes turned to Theo as Francine closed the door behind her.

'If you don't mind, I think I'll go to my room for a little while. Have a rest before we go out for pizza. It's been a tiring day.'

Theo looked at her anxiously. 'You are okay?'

She nodded. 'I'm fine. Lots to think about.'

Once upstairs she sat on the bed and taking the letter out of its envelope she read its short message again.

Dear Agnes,

Please can the two of us meet? Alone. There are certain things I would welcome the opportunity to tell you. I have a coffee every morning at eleven o'clock in the cafe by the entrance to the market. Hope to see you there one morning soon.

Rachel Cortez.

Thoughtfully, Agnes tucked the letter back into the envelope and placed it on the bedside table as her thoughts once again took her unwillingly back to the past...

Fifty-three years ago her life had been very different. Francine, born nine months after the wedding and thought of as a honeymoon baby by everyone, was born after a difficult thirty-eight-hour labour when the doctors gently told her this baby would be her only child. Something she had been secretly glad to learn, having no desire to risk a repetition of those long painful hours. The day she'd arrived home from hospital she'd discovered Oscar had moved into the spare bedroom. Guilt accompanied the feeling of relief that flooded through her body on realising that they wouldn't be sharing a bed. A few weeks later, when the knowledge that Oscar's 'playing away' from home like he had done during her pregnancy and before was continuing, all shreds of guilt disappeared. Life was much easier for her when he was seeing another woman. She knew he had no idea that she was aware of his dalliances, and while she didn't like or condone his behaviour in any way, if it kept him out of her bed she was happy. Serge Cortez at fifty-one was undoubtedly the right age to be the result of one of Oscar's liaisons during that difficult time.

Oscar had taken very little notice of baby Francine. He'd wandered into the bedroom one morning and looked at her sleeping quietly in the crib. 'If only you'd been a boy,' he'd muttered before glaring at Agnes and leaving. A hands-on father in those early days he was not.

It was several months before things settled down into any semblance of a normal life and Agnes could feel she was finally coping. Theo returned from a successful tour and after an awkward first meeting when Agnes felt her heart would break in two, she managed to hide her feelings. To her surprise, when she hesitantly suggested Theo could be one of Francine's godfathers, Oscar agreed.

Theo had played an important part in her and Francine's lives in those days and Agnes would be forever grateful to him for being there for her despite how cruelly she treated him in the end...

Agnes took a deep breath. What to do now though, fifty-odd years later, about this Serge Cortez person? There really was no choice. Rachel Cortez had made a simple enough request to meet her and talk. It could help her to decide whether to do as the notaire wanted and get Francine to do a DNA test or whether to go with her gut feeling that Serge was Oscar's illegitimate son. She had to meet Rachel Cortez. And despite Francine insisting she would go with her, Agnes knew this was something she wanted to do alone.

Decision made, Agnes stood up. Time to get ready to go out for that pizza. When she went downstairs ten minutes later, Theo was sat at the table in the sitting room working on his laptop.

'Shall we have a small aperitif while we wait for Francine?' Theo asked, closing his laptop.

'A tiny one would be good,' Agnes smiled at him. She wandered over to look at the bookcase while he poured the drinks.

'I don't think either of us were surprised at the news this morning, were we?' Agnes said quietly as she studied the titles of the books.

'*Non.* I think if we're honest we were both expecting it. Does the name Rachel Cortez mean anything to you?' Theo said as he handed her a small glass. 'I do not recognise the name Cortez.'

Agnes nodded. 'I had a friend called Rachel once. Not a close, close friend but we had lunch together a few times. I think she rented one of Oscar's properties – maybe it is her? But her surname was Dupont. Perhaps Cortez is her married name.'

'You will go to meet her like she suggests?'

Agnes gave him a rueful look. 'How can I not? But I have every intention of going alone, despite what Francine says. So please don't mention it this evening. I also want to meet Serge. And,' she took a deep breath, 'I think tomorrow morning I'd like to go up to the house. Will you come with me?'

'Of course. You didn't say anything when Francine talked

about going home and then returning in a week or two. Will you go with her if she decides to go?'

Agnes sipped her aperitif. 'I think we need to find out how long things are likely to take – particularly if we go down the DNA route as the notaire wants us to. But no, I don't feel inclined to rush back. Now I'm here, I'd rather like to stay for a while – if that's alright with you?'

'You know you don't even have to ask,' Theo said. 'You can stay forever if you want to.' He gave her an inscrutable smile. Agnes returned it with a small shake of her head. She knew just how much he longed for her to do that.

'Jasmine seems determined to stay down here too. Oh. Now there's something I wasn't expecting to see on your bookshelves.' And Agnes quickly moved away.

'What?' Theo looked at the bookshelves and realised instantly what Agnes had referred to. '*Désolé*. I put it there temporarily, and then forgot to move it.' He reached out and took the urn of ashes off the shelf and placed it out of sight in the built-in cupboard under the stairs.

'We must have a serious talk about what to do with them some time. Perhaps Francine will have an idea?' he said as he closed the cupboard door.

'She's already suggested throwing the ashes in the Med,' Agnes said, laughing. 'Which is as good a suggestion as any, I think. But if Serge Cortez is Oscar's son – and I have this strong feeling that he is – he may want to be involved in deciding.'

When Agnes told Francine later, as the three of them tucked into pizza at a waterside restaurant, that Theo had agreed to accompany her up to the house the next day, she nodded.

'Good. We need to start thinking about clearing out what we can. Come up mid-morning, we can have coffee and then we can go through things together and make a list of the contents. We won't get rid of anything until we know who this Serge Cortez is exactly, and whether he is likely to want a say in how we dispose of things but we can at least get rid of the rubbish and clean the place up a bit.'

22

Strolling through the narrow streets from Lower to Higher Suquet with Theo holding Cerise on her lead the next morning, Agnes suppressed a shiver of apprehension. Oscar was dead, there was nothing he could do to hurt her physically now but what of the hurtful memories that the house itself was likely to stir up in her head? The memory of how helpless and powerless she'd been, unable to stop the things that were happening to her.

Within two or three years her life as Mrs Oscar Agistini had become completely under the control of her husband. Where she went, what she wore, what she ate, what she read, wherever she took Francine, the friends she made – everything she did was decided by Oscar. Perhaps if she hadn't fallen pregnant so quickly, or suffered so badly from morning sickness she would have been more alert to what started to happen during those nine months and took over her life afterwards. Although whether she would have been strong enough to stop his coercive behaviour was doubtful.

As Theo opened the front door and called out '*Bonjour* Francine', Agnes took a deep breath. It was just a house that she'd lived in a long time ago. The memories of that time needed to stay buried deep in the life of the woman she'd been then, not upset the woman she now was. She'd pretend all the mental cruelty, all the physical hurt, had happened to another person in this house, someone separate from her. Someone she didn't know. She was, after all, a different person now. She'd walk in and view the house dispassionately like a stranger would. After all, she hadn't been here for so long she was a stranger.

'I'm in the kitchen,' Francine called out. 'Come on through.'

The kitchen had been modernised and Agnes breathed a relieved sigh. So different to how it had been as to be unrecognisable to her and she happily sat at the kitchen table to drink the coffee Francine made her.

'Jasmine not here?' Agnes asked.

'She's upstairs working,' Francine said. 'She'll probably be down later.'

After coffee, Francine picked up a notebook and pencil and the three of them started to move through the house. The memories came slowly to Agnes at first. Disjointed from each other. The furniture in the sitting room had changed but in amongst it there were a couple of pieces from the past. The bureau where Oscar had dealt with the paperwork for his property business was still in the same place, pushed back against the wall, a well-worn briefcase leaning against it. A MacBook Air laptop sat on its leather writing surface. Agnes recognised the wing chair in front of the bureau, it had been upstairs in the main bedroom.

A large leather settee was placed directly in front of the inbuilt log fire, cutting the room in half and blocking free movement. The shelves on the left-hand side of the fireplace had been removed, replaced by a single shelf, wide enough to take the television that stood on it. The right-hand side bookshelves were still there but empty save for a few boating magazines and a couple of old paperbacks. Nothing in the room ruffled Agnes's equilibrium. The dispassionate stranger persona she'd taken on temporarily remained calm.

'Do we have to go through all this paperwork?' Francine said standing by the bureau and opening a few drawers. She rifled through some files in the top drawer. 'There's a file here with your family name on it, Maman. Oh, there's also a large envelope marked "For the attention of Agnes Agistini". Wonder what that is?' Francine held it out to Agnes. 'Do you want to open it now?'

Agnes, uneasy about what the contents might be, shook her head. She'd rather open it in private later. 'Leave it there for now. I'll collect it later as we leave.'

'The rest of the files are probably a mixture of business and personal stuff,' Theo said, joining Francine at the bureau. 'Oscar closed the business when he finally retired about six years ago, but there's still the occasional official paper showing up and needing to be signed. It's difficult to work here in France after retirement and he said it wasn't worth the hassle.'

'Hopefully it won't be too difficult or take too long to go through,' Francine said.

'Would you like me to go through them for you?' Theo said. 'It would probably be easier for me to do it.'

'*Merci*, Theo, I accept that offer.' Agnes breathed a sigh of relief as they all left the room and made their way upstairs. There had been no horrible memories rushing to the surface in there.

Francine opened the door of the bedroom she was using. 'Just the furniture in here really. The wardrobes and cupboards are empty – apart from my stuff of course. Now for Oscar's bedroom,' she continued and walked along the hallway. Francine saw Agnes glance at the remaining closed door. 'He appears to have shut that room off years ago.' She glanced at Theo who nodded.

'He never said why he stopped using it,' he shrugged. 'Simply said he preferred the other one.'

Agnes pulled the door open a few inches and peered inside. The dispassionate stranger resolve wobbled as she gazed at the neglected room. A room that she'd spent so many unhappy hours in, trying to find a way forward. There was no need to step over the threshold of this room so she didn't. Carefully she closed the door and followed Theo and Francine to the final room.

'I'm sorry, I meant to strip the bed and wash everything before you came up to the house,' Francine said.

'It doesn't matter,' Agnes said, gazing around the room. It was just a bedroom, no sinister vibes stirring things up in her mind. She slowly crossed to the bureau and looked at the French mirror standing there. Agnes looked at Francine.

'Do you remember how much you loved polishing this with me?' Turning her attention back to the mirror she said. 'It was my grandmère's and I used to keep all my jewellery in the secret drawers. I also hid some money in it whenever I could but there was never enough.' Agnes sighed, remembering how hard it had been to even save a few francs out of the housekeeping Oscar gave her. He was always asking to see receipts. If it hadn't been for Theo she'd never have got away.

'They're not really secret drawers though, are they?' Francine said as she pulled first one and then the other open. 'They aren't very deep either.'

'Oh, that's not the secret bit,' Agnes said. 'You take them both out,' and reaching to the back of the gap she felt around. 'This is the secret bit, if it works after all this time. Voila,' and as she pressed the side of the framework inside around the base the back fell open revealing an empty cavity. A memory of keeping the Celtic necklace hidden in there for years, never daring to wear it in public, slipped into her mind. Even when she was living in England, it had taken years before she'd taken it out of her small jewellery pouch and started to wear it regularly. In those early days, the memories it provoked were just too sad for her to contemplate. She put the drawers back in place.

'I think technically this belongs to me anyway as it was my grandmère's so I think I'd like to have it,' Agnes said.

'I don't think anyone will argue with you over that,' Francine said, reaching out for the comb on the bureau. 'Shall we take this ready to go to the notaire? It has a few hairs in it.'

'No. Let's leave it until we have a date for the next rendez-vous,' Agnes said. 'We know where it is.'

'Do you want to go up to the attic room?' Theo asked.

Agnes shook her head. '*Non*. I don't think there is any need and Jasmine is working up there. No point in disturbing her.' The attic had never been converted in her day there was little point in her seeing it now.

23

Over the next few days the four of them settled into, not exactly a routine, but a definite French way of living. Theo had his daily habits, croissants and coffee first thing, a walk along the harbour and then up to the Marché Forville for the day's food before returning to the cottage and planning the rest of the day. Agnes soon found herself drawn into the rhythm of his life. A rhythm of living she'd forgotten existed but one she drew pleasure from and was enjoying living.

Life for Francine and Zazz too was slowly evolving into a distinct pattern. Zazz ran every morning, usually meeting up with Mel, before returning with the croissants for breakfast, which they ate together companionably, if silently, in the kitchen. One morning Mel went back with her for breakfast after their run and Zazz introduced her to Francine.

'Mel's dad owns the cafe where we had coffee a couple of mornings ago,' Zazz said, putting fresh croissants on a plate. Francine, pouring coffees, turned to look at Mel.

'You're Piers's daughter, Armelle?'

'Nobody ever calls me that but yeah, that's me. You know my papa?'

'A long time ago,' Francine smiled. 'Your maman too. Do you work in the cafe like your brothers?'

'Sometimes if it's busy like at festival time but I'm busy with my own business in summer.'

'Mel manages some holiday lets,' Zazz said. 'She's keeping an ear out for somewhere for me to rent, in case I can't stay here.' She looked at her mother, hoping to goad her into answering.

'Something Granny and I still have to discuss,' Francine said. Determined not to be drawn into a row in front of Mel.

'I had a glass of wine with Piers on his boat the other evening,' she said. 'It's a beautiful boat – do you sail?'

Mel laughed. 'That boat is Papa's mid-life crisis *cadeau* to himself. *Mais oui*, Papa taught us all to sail. I try to go out for a sail with him every week. Zazz, if you sail you might like to come at the weekend?'

'I'm a dinghy girl, not used to proper yachts,' Zazz said, laughing.

'Sails are sails, some are just bigger than others,' Mel grinned at her, before picking up her coffee and finishing it. 'I'd better go. Lots to do today. Thank you for breakfast.'

'I'll see you tomorrow,' Zazz said and went to the door to say goodbye.

Left alone, Francine stared out at the neglected courtyard through the kitchen window wondering if it was worth the effort of cleaning it up and making it user friendly again. If Zazz was going to stay here for at least a few weeks, it would be a useful outdoor space. Having it clear and clean for house viewings when the house went on the market would be good too.

'Penny for them?' Zazz said, returning. 'You look miles away.'

'Thinking about the courtyard. Whether it's worth clearing it out and eating out there.'

'Shouldn't take long,' Zazz said. 'I planned on doing it for Oscar when I moved in. But I suppose it depends on how long you're going to let me stay here.'

'If you stay at all,' Francine said sharply. 'Although Granny doesn't seem to be in a hurry to make another rendez-vous with the notaire or to kickstart the DNA tests that sound inevitable.' She hesitated. 'I honestly thought we'd come over, see the notaire, start clearing the house, have a bit of a holiday and then go home. I was not expecting a complication called Serge Cortez.'

'Granny didn't seem that surprised though, did she?' Zazz said quietly.

Francine gave her a sharp look. 'What d'you mean?'

'Didn't you see her after she asked that one question, how old is he? She simply nodded thoughtfully, as if his age meant something to her.'

Francine was silent for a few seconds. 'My father wasn't the best of fathers and he certainly wasn't the most faithful of husbands. As for being the kindly grandfather you seem to think he would have been if you'd met him years ago there never was a chance of that happening.'

'Mum, I know that,' Zazz said. 'But I did have the right to meet him and make up my own mind about him.'

Francine gave her a questioning look. 'And have you?'

'Honestly? The couple of times I met him I thought he was a very manipulative man. Charming when he wanted to be but I'm glad I never crossed him, which I probably would have done living here, if he hadn't died.'

'Yes, you probably would have clashed – luckily you didn't get to find out just how evil a man he was.'

'Mum, that's a bit strong. Evil?'

'No, it's not. In fact it sums him up perfectly.' Francine took a deep breath. 'Right, what are we up to today?'

Zazz, realising that the conversation about Oscar had been closed down yet again said. 'I'm going to edit a piece I've written for Marcus about how there's more to Cannes than a film festival, send it and hope he likes it. Then I'm going to finish another feature about the monks on Saint Honorat for my blog. You?'

Francine's phone buzzed at that moment with an incoming e-mail which she quickly read. 'I'm going to be working too,' she said, looking up at Zazz. 'Urgent edit and proofread needed. They want to know if I can do it within two days. Glad I brought my laptop. I'll e-mail them straight away to send it through.'

'See you later then,' Zazz said. 'I'll drop Gran and Theo a text to let them know we'll see them at lunchtime.'

24

When Zazz told Agnes that Francine was going to be busy working up at Oscar's for the next day or two she realised she had been given a perfect opportunity to make contact with Rachel Cortez on her own, without Francine wanting to go with her. Theo, after she'd told him her plan, insisted he would accompany her to the cafe rendez-vous and stay nearby but leave her to meet Rachel alone. 'To use Francine's phrase, it's non-negotiable, I'm coming with you,' he told her.

Agnes and Theo with Cerise on her lead, left the house just before eleven o'clock to make their way to the Marché Forville. 'Did Rachel give you any identification clues?' Theo asked. 'If you did know her in the past, you'll maybe recognise her but if not...' his voice trailed away.

'No, she didn't mention she'd be carrying a red handbag, wearing a hat or clutching a certain flower,' Agnes said laughing. 'But I'm sure somehow we'll manage to connect.'

The cafe when they reached it was busy with occupied tables with two or more people sitting at them. At first glance there didn't appear to be a table with a single customer but then Agnes spotted one tucked away in the far corner with a lone woman watching the door. As she saw Agnes the woman smiled and gave a half wave.

'She's at the back. I'll see you in a bit,' Agnes said and began to make her way towards the woman. As she got closer she recognised her old friend from the past, Rachel Dupont.

'*Bonjour*,' Agnes said, pulling out a chair and joining Rachel at the table. 'I wondered if it was you. It's been a long time.'

'*Oui*. We were young then, now we are old,' Rachel answered.

'It would be nice to say we haven't changed a bit but we both know that wouldn't be true,' Agnes said with a smile.

The waiter appeared at their table. '*Madame*, you would like?' he asked looking at Agnes.

'Un cappuccino, *s'il vous plaît*.' She glanced at Rachel's almost empty cup. 'Another?'

Rachel nodded. '*Merci*.'

As the waiter moved away to fetch their order, Rachel looked at Agnes. 'Before we go any further, you need to know that whilst I regret certain of my past actions, I don't regret having my son, Serge.'

Agnes returned her look steadily. 'I hope for your sake he is nothing like his father.'

'He isn't,' Rachel said quietly. 'His adoptive father was the main male influence in his life – and he was a good man.'

'That's good. I do have a few questions I need to ask you,' Agnes said. 'The first one is, how long were you involved with Oscar?'

'It started before you were married and carried on afterwards. Your daughter was about a year old when I fell pregnant and Oscar literally threw me out.'

Agnes went to speak but the waiter was back and she stopped as he carefully placed their drinks in front of them.

'If he hadn't thrown you out, would you have carried on the liaison?' she asked when he'd left.

Rachel shook her head. 'No. It was too toxic a situation for a child to be involved in.'

'So, how did you even get entangled with Oscar?'

'You know I lived in one of his rental apartments? In those days Oscar collected the rent himself. One week when he knocked on the door I had to tell him I'd started a new job and I wouldn't have the money until I got paid at the end of the following week. I remember the assessing look he gave me for ooh, about thirty seconds, before he told me to bring it to the house the Friday evening of that week at nine o'clock. I thanked him and he left.' Rachel sipped her cappuccino. 'You can guess what happened that Friday evening when I took him the rent money. And that was the beginning – at least I got to live rent free for eighteen months.'

Agnes spooned the froth from the top of her coffee before picking up her cup and drinking some of the hot liquid, waiting for Rachel to continue.

'When you and he married I thought it would finish and I would be free of him but *non*, Oscar said there was no reason to stop. And he knew by then how much I depended on living rent-free.' Rachel looked at Agnes.

'What I did was wrong, but I know for a fact that I wasn't his only woman in all that time,' she said quietly.

Agnes gave her a sad smile. 'There were always women in his life. I take it when you became pregnant he wasn't happy? Did he help at all?'

Rachel made a choking sound. 'First thing he asked me – was I sure it was his? When I told him there was no doubt about it, he told me to either get rid of it or to get out of his apartment. He refused to acknowledge any responsibility.'

'I remember hearing that you'd suddenly gone to live in Italy. Ventimiglia, I think.'

Rachel nodded. 'There was no way I could have an abortion. My sister lived there and she took me in. Helped me. When Serge was nearly three, I met and fell in love with Antonio Cortez who, happily for me, was more than willing to take Serge on as his own child.' Rachel's eyes misted over. 'We had a good marriage. Serge has two sisters whom he adores. Sadly, Antonio, he die two years ago.'

'I'm sorry to hear that,' Agnes said.

'I come back to live in Cannes. Serge still lives in Italy. Inevitably I suppose, I bumped into Oscar. He asked what I'd done about the baby. When I told him I'd had a baby boy he asked if it was too late for him to meet his son. I told him far too late. Not only had he missed out on his son but he also had a grown-up grandson he'd never met. He said he felt bad about the way he'd treated me and his son but he would make amends when he died. Leave them both something in the will.'

'Did you believe him?'

Rachel shrugged. 'I wanted to but I had to trust he would remember. I didn't say anything to Serge when I heard Oscar had died unexpectedly, simply waited for the notaire to contact me. He didn't. So I knew Oscar hadn't done the things he said he would. I made a rendez-vous to see Monsieur Caumont and he confirmed there was no mention of Serge in the will. It was then I asked to sign an affidavit naming Oscar as Serge's papa knowing that the notaire would have to take that seriously. Gave me a huge lecture about the consequences of lying under oath.' Rachel shook her head. 'I haven't lied. But he said he could do nothing until he had spoken to you and the family which was why I left the letter with him to give to you.'

'I'm pleased you did. I think it better that we talk together away from the notaire. I have no illusions about the kind of man Oscar was. The two of us have both suffered at his hands.' Agnes paused. 'Both literally and physically,' she added quietly and gave Rachel a sad smile as she nodded in agreement.

'I am sorry I create a problem for you at this time,' Rachel said. 'But I believe and hope you would want the right thing to be done finally for Serge.'

Agnes nodded. 'Yes. But first I want to meet Serge and his son so how do you feel about the seven of us meeting for aperitifs one evening and getting to know each other a little?'

When Rachel nodded, Agnes pulled out her phone. 'Give me your number and I'll message you the address. Would next Friday night at six thirty suit you?'

'Yes,' Rachel said and called out the number for Agnes to add it to her contacts.

'*Bon.* Organised,' Agnes said. 'We'll talk more then.'

Theo was waiting by the wine cave at the side of the market as Agnes and Rachel left the cafe together. Rachel smiled. 'That's Oscar's brother, isn't it? Was he afraid you and I have an argument?'

'I think he was a little worried for me,' Agnes said. 'He, like your Antonio, is one of the good men.'

She smiled at Theo. 'You didn't have to wait. But thank you.'

They both said goodbye to Rachel and she left to walk in the opposite direction down rue Meyandier. Walking back to the cottage with Theo, Agnes told him about inviting Rachel and her family for aperitifs. 'I hope you don't mind me inviting strangers to your cottage?'

'*Non. C'est bon.* I too look forward to meeting Rachel's son and grandson.'

Francine was already at the cottage preparing lunch for them all when they got back. 'Hi, hope you've had a good morning. Been out exploring?'

'Not really,' Agnes said. 'I met with Rachel Cortez and we had a good conversation.'

Francine stopped mixing the oil and vinegar dressing she was making for the green salad she'd prepared to accompany the cold chicken breasts for lunch and looked at her mother.

'I can't believe you went behind my back and met that woman on your own,' Francine said. 'You knew I wanted to go with you.'

'And I wanted to meet her alone. Theo understood that. I don't know what you thought was likely to happen between us,' Agnes answered.

'I didn't think anything was likely to happen, I simply wanted to meet her too. She is the mother of this unknown half-brother I appear to have acquired.'

'You'll get to meet her soon – with Serge and Albert, her grandson. The three of them are coming for aperitifs here next Friday evening.'

'What fun,' Zazz said, arriving at that moment ready for lunch.

Francine gave her mother an exasperated look. 'Oh, that's just great. Wouldn't it be better to all meet formally at the notaire's office the first time?'

Agnes shook her head. 'Informal is better.' She looked at Francine and decided a change of subject was necessary. 'Have you spoken to Edwin recently?'

'We text every day but haven't spoken for a day or two. He's been busy.'

'Why don't you ask him to come out and join us,' Agnes said. 'I think we're going to be here for at least another week, if not ten days. And he did say he would be coming out.'

'I thought we'd get the will business sorted and at least start to clear the house so that we could relax. And now I've got this urgent work to do and we haven't even decided what to do with the ashes yet,' Francine said, agitatedly running her hand through her hair.

Agnes waved her hand in the air. 'It will all fall into place. I've decided too that Jasmine can stay in the house like she planned. Won't be forever of course because it's going to be sold at some point but for now, there's really no reason why she shouldn't stay on there when we go home. It's better to have someone living in it rather than having it empty.'

'Thanks so much, Gran,' Zazz said, moving across to give her gran a hug.

Francine stared at her mother for several seconds. 'You're very laissez-faire suddenly about this whole situation. I don't understand why.'

Agnes took a deep breath. 'Meeting Rachel today was a cathartic experience for me. It finally sank in that Oscar is dead. He is personally never going to bother me or you again. Realising that gave me an immense feeling of relief. I'd even say it makes me happy. And if that makes me a bad person...' Agnes gave a half shrug.

There was silence as both Theo and Francine stared at her before Theo moved and took her in his arms and held her tight.

'It makes you a very human person,' he said softly before pressing a kiss against her temple.

25

Zazz smiled as she and Francine walked back up together to Oscar's house after lunch. 'I'm so relieved that Granny has said yes to me staying in the house,' Zazz said. 'Once I've finished my piece for Marcus and sent it I'll make a start on the yard.'

Francine glanced at her. 'Was it your idea to come to live in France for a few months? Or did Oscar put the idea into your head?'

'I fell in love with the place on my first visit,' Zazz said. 'I know it sounds silly but it felt like I was in a place I could call home. Maybe it's in my DNA because of you and Granny.'

'Did you say that to Oscar?'

Zazz shook her head. 'Not directly, no. But once I'd met Mel I did start to talk to her about the possibility. He overheard me once asking her advice about how easy it would be, where I could live, what I could do. He immediately said finding somewhere to live was sorted because I could live with him. And that's when I began to seriously believe it was do-able.'

'Don't get too comfortable because the house will have to be sold,' Francine warned.

'Mel is talking about the two of us sharing a small apartment so hopefully by the time the house sells that will be happening.'

'How does Rufus feel about you staying down here for months?'

'Rufus and I broke up. He's off to America soon with a new job.'

'How d'you feel about that?' Francine asked gently. 'I thought you two were good together. And why didn't you mention it?'

'I've mentioned it now,' Zazz shrugged. 'I was hurt by the way it happened but I'm not devastated. I never truly thought we'd be together for ever and ever, so.' Zazz pulled a face. 'At least I can concentrate on growing my social media presence and living down here.'

'I honestly don't understand how being a social media influencer can be a full-time job,' Francine said.

'I have to plan my content, research brands that will be of interest to my followers. It's all a question of putting good content out that people want to see, buy or be involved with,' she paused. 'I'm looking forward to meeting Serge and family,' Zazz said, glancing at her mum.

'I can't say I am,' Francine said, accepting the change of subject. 'I'm too old to suddenly have a half-brother thrust upon me.'

'I'm quite looking forward to having another uncle.' Zazz laughed as she saw the look on Francine's face. 'Even if he's only a half one. And a half-cousin too.'

'Never thought I'd be part of a dysfunctional family,' Francine muttered.

'It might be fun. Anyway, living in different countries you're not exactly going to be bosom buddies in daily contact with each other, are you?'

Francine shook her head. 'True but it feels weird.'

Edwin phoned as they let themselves into the house. Zazz called out a 'Hi, Dad' before disappearing upstairs and Francine went through to the kitchen to talk and update him on what was happening.

'I wish you were here. Maman seems to think we're going to be here for at least another week or ten days. And Zazz has dropped the bombshell news that she's planning on living down here for the foreseeable. Have you decided when you're coming out? Maybe you can talk some sense into her. And I do miss you. We can have a mini break together.'

'That's why I'm ringing. I've managed to get everything done and cleared my desk for a week. I've already booked my ticket,' Edwin said. 'I'll have to bring my laptop but I'll be with you next Friday afternoon.'

Francine breathed a sigh of relief. 'That's brilliant news. Especially as Maman has invited the three Cortez's for aperitifs that evening. Zazz is talking to me a little but she has a new friend so is off out a lot of the time – she and Rufus have broken up by the way. Agnes and Theo are doing things together. I must put my mind to starting the house clearance too.'

'Leave the house until I get there and I'll give you a hand,' Edwin said.

'I think I'll do that, especially as I've now got some urgent editing and proofreading to do for work. I've met up with an old friend too, Piers. He's got a cafe in town and he owns the most beautiful boat. I had a glass of wine with him on board the other evening, I can't wait to introduce the two of you. I think you'll get on.'

'Look forward to meeting him. I'd better let you go. Give my love to Zazz and Agnes. My arrival time on the Friday is about four fifteen. Love you.'

'Love you too. See you soon,' and Francine ended the call

feeling a lot happier knowing that Edwin was coming to join them. She'd concentrate on getting her editing dealt with and then when Edwin got here they could tackle clearing the house together. And for the first time she could show him the sights of her hometown. Something she realised she was going to enjoy.

* * *

It took Zazz less than an hour to sweep and wash the yard down and clean the patio set later that afternoon. Next, she weeded the plant tubs with lemon trees, roses and a crimson bougainvillea, before giving them all a good soaking that they looked to be in dire need of. Job done. Supper under the stars could be on the agenda from now on.

Francine was in the kitchen writing a shopping list when Zazz went back indoors. 'Dad is coming on Friday, isn't that great?' she said. 'Thought I'd better get some food in. We can't keep eating out or going down to Theo's. In fact, we can have them up here for dinner.' She stopped when she saw the look on Zazz's face. 'Or maybe not, the way Maman feels about this house. But I can take stuff down and cook it at Theo's. Can't expect him to feed all of us all the time.'

'I'm eating with Mel tonight,' Zazz said. 'I think too now that you know, and I know I'm staying in the house, I need to try and get my work and life routine sorted for when you've left. I have to remember I'm not on holiday. Maybe just meet up with you guys a couple of nights a week instead of lunch every day as well as dinner?' She looked at Francine, hoping that she would understand her need to get her new life organised and not just drift around.

'I understand what you're saying and why but now that Dad will be joining us at the weekend, it would be good to eat *en famille* whilst he is here?' Francine said. 'Once we leave you'll be on your own.'

'Okay. Breakfast every day together and then let the day's plans decide about dinner,' Zazz said.

'So tomorrow?'

'Tomorrow Mel has suggested I shadow her for the day and maybe get some ideas for features and content for my Instagram, so we'll probably get lunch somewhere and then in the evening I've planned on going to the cinema.' Zazz smiled at her mum. 'And Friday night is out as the Cortez's are coming.'

'You certainly seem to be settling in down here. Mel seems a good friend already.'

'She certainly is.'

'So how about Saturday night dinner somewhere nice with everyone?' Francine said.

'Cool. Sounds like a plan. Enjoy your shopping. See you later.' And Zazz disappeared upstairs to her room.

26

When Zazz ran down rue Saint Antoine and crossed the road making for the Allées de la Liberté the next morning she could see Mel already waiting for her by the statue of the Englishman, Lord Brougham.

'I love this part of Cannes,' Zazz said, looking at the statue and the water feature in front of it and the people milling around. 'I wonder what he would think about history calling him the father of Cannes. Would he even recognise the place now?'

Mel laughed. 'I doubt it and definitely not in the next few weeks.' Zazz gave her a puzzled look.

'The Film Festival begins soon and the place will go a little mad. The hoardings are already going up all over town. Cleaning the red carpet will be next.'

'I'd forgotten about the festival,' Zazz admitted.

'Have you been down on a Sunday morning yet when there's a brocante and artisan market here? *Non*? You should, lots of ideas and people to interview for features,' Mel said.

'Maybe next Sunday,' Zazz said. 'Where are we going first today?'

'An apartment on rue d'Antibes. It's one I've just taken on the management of and I need to check it out. The first rentals are due in tomorrow.'

Ten minutes later, after Mel had introduced Zazz to the concierge, they were in a lift going up to the sixth floor of a large apartment block. Stepping out on to a hallway with several doors on either side, Mel made for one near the end of the hallway and unlocked the door.

'This apartment is quite luxurious. There's a sitting room, two bedrooms, bathroom, kitchen and balcony, and,' Mel said, opening the patio doors onto the balcony and stepping out, 'a sea view out over the Croisette. I think this is going to be a popular rental with my clients. Now, the cleaner was here yesterday so let's check she's done a good job. Everything has to be spotless, so we need to check this list.'

It was twenty minutes before Mel declared everything to be to her satisfaction and they locked up the apartment and left. 'You do this for every apartment every time it's rented?' Zazz asked.

Mel nodded. 'And when there are three or four changeovers on the same day, it gets pretty busy.'

'I can imagine,' Zazz said.

'I'm slowly building up a really good team of cleaners though and that's half the battle. The next apartment is in an old Belle Epoque villa about two streets away. Come on, there's a good cafe nearby, we can get a spot of lunch afterwards.'

Zazz fell in love with the ground-floor apartment in the Belle Epoque villa as Mel opened the door. 'I love this. The other apartment was lovely but this has so much more character. You can feel the history of the place.' She looked around at the high ceilings, the chandeliers in the sitting room and in the two bedrooms, the French doors leading out to the garden, the bathroom with its old-fashioned free-standing bath and the kitchen, modern but yet traditional with only its cooking range on view, all other modern appliances hidden behind custom made wooden doors. 'If I came on holiday here, I'd never want to leave.'

'This is the last season it's going to be a holiday rental. The owners have decided to rent it out permanently from September,' Mel said. 'They've asked me if I would be interested in renting it but I'd need someone to share with me.'

Mel gave Zazz a quick look. 'Are you likely to still be here in September? If you are would you be interested in sharing this place with me? I'd rather share with someone I know.'

'Seriously?' Zazz stared at her. 'You're asking me if I'd like to live here in this wonderful apartment with you?'

'Well, your grandfather's house will be sold and you have to live somewhere if you do stay.'

'I'm definitely staying,' Zazz said. 'I need to live in this house.'

'*Bon*,' Mel smiled. 'And if you need to earn extra money maybe you can help me meet and greet rentals on changeover days here in Cannes when I'm stretched with too many?'

'I'd enjoy doing that,' Zazz said. She twirled around looking at the sitting room they were standing in. 'Will it come with all this furniture?' Somewhat traditional in design the furniture fitted the room perfectly.

'*Oui*.'

Zazz sighed happily.

'We'd better get on. I need to buy some baskets for the welcome gifts I fill on behalf of the owners to make their guests feel welcome.'

The rest of the day passed swiftly with visits to various shops to buy soaps, wine, olive oil and some handmade chocolates. Zazz helped Mel carry everything back to her studio before saying goodbye and going home to get ready for the cinema that evening.

Zazz hummed happily to herself as she stood under the shower. She could hardly believe that Mel had asked her to share that wonderful apartment with her from September. She'd work hard this summer, adding as much money as she could to her savings to give herself a cushion over winter. Life down here in the South of France was looking good.

* * *

Theo and Agnes were clearing the breakfast things away when Theo said. 'I thought I'd go up to the house this morning and start to go through Oscar's files and papers. See if there is anything we need to do. Is that okay with you and do you want to come?'

'No. I'm going to try and find a hairdresser who has open appointments and doesn't need me to make a rendez-vous,' Agnes said. 'If it's not too much trouble could you bring my grandmère's dressing mirror back with you?'

'*Bien sûr.*'

When Theo reached the house Francine was in the kitchen engrossed in the manuscript she had open on her laptop.

'I've come up to make a start on sorting the files and papers in the bureau. I won't disturb you. Oh,' he said, 'can I have that empty box?' pointing to one in the corner. Francine nodded and he picked it up and made his way into the sitting room.

He gave the few pieces of paper he found in the briefcase a quick look before deciding they were in order and could be placed in the 'keep for seven years just in case' box that he was about to create. He saw the envelope with Agnes's name on it that Francine had pointed out and Agnes had failed to collect on the bureau top and placed that in the briefcase.

Next, he started on the files. The one Francine had seen with

Agnes's family name on it didn't contain anything unusual, just out-of-date papers relating to the time when she'd lived in the house. Why Oscar had them at all was a mystery and Theo put them in the throw away pile. As he'd expected, the other files were mostly old business files that Oscar had never bothered to put away, so after a cursory glance, in the box to be kept they went. The next file he picked up was bulkier than the others and the name on it startled him.

Denice Bernard. Why on earth would Oscar have a file on Agnes's long-lost sister?

Theo sat down on the nearby armchair and started to go through the papers inside the file. Twenty minutes later he gave a deep groan and leant back with his eyes closed, muttering a string of expletives, '*Bâtarde. Connard. Bâtarde*', under his breath. His unscrupulous brother had outdone himself this time and Theo had no idea how he was going to tell Agnes about the latest crime that his brother had committed against her.

Sighing, he closed the file and placed it in the briefcase alongside the envelope. Theo glanced at the envelope, sorely tempted to take a look inside and see if that contained another problem for Agnes. But the envelope was sealed and Theo knew he would have to wait to learn what further misfortune for Agnes was likely to be inside.

One thing was certain, he wasn't going to give either the file or the envelope to Agnes today. He had no idea what the envelope contained but he'd count on it not being good news. Agnes had enough to deal with right now. He would hang on to both the envelope and the file and choose his moment carefully and make sure he was at her side when she opened them.

* * *

Agnes, wandering through Cannes on her own for the first time since they arrived, found her thoughts drifting back to the time when the streets had been so familiar to her. Today she realised it would be easy for her to get lost. Diversion after diversion was set up already to allow lorries to unload barriers and other street furniture in preparation for the upcoming film festival.

So many memories of wandering around at festival time with Denice began to flood into her mind. Denice always seemed to know the places to go to see the stars and Agnes was happy to go with her. Agnes had barely left the house during the first film festival after Denice had disappeared, and when she did venture out, she couldn't stop the tears flowing. It wasn't the same without her sister excitedly pointing out the various actors who were in town. She'd missed her so much.

Agnes turned on to rue d'Antibes hoping to find a hairdresser somewhere along its length, when the memory of the very last time she'd been in town for the festival fell into her mind...

Oscar was away on business and Theo had been in town for a few days. The two of them had taken an excited six-year-old Francine down to the Palais des Festivals to see if they could spot Elizabeth Montgomery, the American actress who played Samantha in Francine's favourite show Bewitched. *They were strolling along with Francine between them holding a hand each, trying to dodge the crowds, when Agnes suddenly felt uncomfortable, as if she was being watched. She turned around and saw a woman arm in arm with a man in a small crowd several metres behind, staring at the three of them.*

Quickly Agnes let go of Francine's hand. 'Theo, stay with Francine for me. There's something, someone, I need to check out.'

But when she turned around again the crowd around the couple had increased and she could barely see them. Frantically Agnes tried to push her way past people, apologising as she elbowed them out of her way. As she reached the outer edge of the crowd, she saw the couple climb into one of the waiting limousines outside the Palais des Festivals. She watched as the door slammed and the driver whisked them away.

Agnes let out a deep breath of disappointment and walked back slowly to rejoin Francine and Theo. She couldn't be sure the elegant woman with the red hair was Denice, she hadn't been able to get close enough to see her face properly. But her gut instinct was saying, 'who else would have stared at us like that?' It must have been Denice.

'Where did you go, Maman?' Francine asked. 'Did you see Samantha?'

'No, I'm sorry, I didn't see Samantha. I thought I saw someone I knew, but I was wrong,' Agnes said...

As the short memory faded away, Agnes realised she'd stopped outside a hairdresser's. Somebody was leaving and smiled at Agnes as they held the door open for her. 'Best hair-dressers in town if you're hesitating,' the woman said.

Agnes smiled and took the handle of the open door, 'Thank you,' and walked in hoping the woman was right.

27

It was gone nine o'clock and the sun was setting when Francine finished her final read through of the manuscript she'd been working on. Once she'd pressed the button and emailed it to the publisher, she switched off her laptop, stood up, stretching her arms above her head and rolled her shoulders, trying to ease the tension in them.

Zazz had returned from her day with Mel and Francine had wished her a good evening when she'd briefly popped into the kitchen for a drink of water before she left for the cinema. Francine had cried off from having dinner with Agnes and Theo, blaming pressure of work, which was true. But now she was seriously hungry. Frites. That was what she fancied. So that was what she was going to have.

Francine grabbed her denim jacket and ten minutes later was clutching an extra-large portion of frites as she walked along the harbour quay. Piers was standing in the stern of his boat talking to a young man and she gave him a happy smile and prepared to walk on by, not wanting to interrupt.

'Frankie. Come and meet my youngest son, Andre. Would you like a glass of wine to go with those frites?'

'If the two of you are busy I don't want to get in the way,' Francine said.

'*Enchanté*, Madame Mansell,' Andre said as Piers introduced them. 'I am leaving. I'm off to meet some friends at the Martinez,' and he leapt out of the boat cockpit onto the quay and with a wave of his hand was gone. 'See you later, Papa.'

Piers helped Francine on board and then fetched two glasses and a bottle of wine.

'Want to share my frites?' Francine offered.

'I thought you'd never offer,' Piers said, laughing.

Sitting there on the gently moving yacht, enjoying the warm night air, sipping a cool glass of wine and sharing the bag of frites with Piers, Francine gave a short laugh.

'This is so weird. Technically, I suppose you could say I'm here on a short break, a mini holiday, while we sort out the will. I'm not a local. But I'm not a real holidaymaker either. I feel so at home sitting here with you. None of this,' she waved her hand in the general direction of the restaurants and bars lining the other side of the quay, 'is strange or new to me. I remember it from an earlier time – granted, it's a lot smarter than it used to be. The years I've been away have seemingly disappeared. Right now, I feel as though I'm back living in Cannes as if I'd never left. And I'm surprised I feel so happy to be back.'

Piers took a frite and ate it thoughtfully. 'You were born in this town, *n'est-ce pas*? I think you feel like this, it is because in your heart, you are a French woman, not the uptight English woman you have turned into.'

Shocked, Francine turned to look at him. She remembered in the past you could always rely on Piers not to hold back on his opinions. It seemed nothing had changed. 'You think I am uptight?'

Piers nodded. 'I remember you being so carefree and adventurous. Of course, life changes us all as we grow older. We have to work hard to remember our true selves are still inside us when we stop being known simply as Piers, or Francine and become someone different in the world. Wife, maman, husband, papa. Our old selves get swallowed up by our new identities and if we're not careful our true, younger, version is lost. One has to dig deep to remember the dreams and hopes of a younger you. I think you have lost that.'

Francine gave him a rueful smile. 'When did you get to be so wise and enlightened?'

'You have to trust me on this. I spent a long time finding the true me again when Mimi left.' Piers said. '*La joie de vivre* – the joy of life is everything, Frankie. And I think you have lost it.'

They sat in a companionable silence as they finished the frites and drank their rosé. Piers broke the silence when he fetched the bottle of wine and topped up their glasses.

'I know someone who is interested in Oscar's boat.'

Francine sighed. 'I forgot to ask Theo about the boat. Give me the name and contact details and I'll pass them on to Theo. He's the best person to deal with it, neither Maman nor I know anything about boats or the process of selling them.' She picked up her glass and took a sip.

'Edwin is arriving on Friday and in the evening we're meeting my potential half-brother, his son and also his mother. Zazz is looking forward to possibly having a new uncle, a new cousin. I only wish I was half as excited as she is at the thought of meeting them.'

'See, there you go again,' Piers said. 'Uptight. Be more Zazz-like. Relax and treat him like a potential new friend. If you don't get on you don't have to see him again. If you do, well, you might have fun.'

Francine laughed. 'I'll try. I met your Mel the other morning. She's lovely. Zazz and her have gone to the cinema together tonight. I'm so pleased Zazz has found a good friend.'

Piers gave her an amused smile as he shook his head. 'It's true Zazz has gone to the cinema tonight but not with Mel. She's gone with my eldest son, Dominic.'

28

Theo and Agnes went to the market on Friday morning to buy some cheeses, nuts, olives, sourdough bread, tapenade and a *pissaladière*, ready for the evening's aperitifs. They also went to the wine cave where Theo helped Agnes choose the champagne she wanted to serve. Leaving the market, Theo insisted he had to have something sweet with his coffee this morning and they stopped at the boulangerie and bought two apricot tarts.

Back at the cottage Agnes organised coffee, put the tarts on plates and carried everything out to the yard while Theo put the shopping away.

'Do you want to come this afternoon when I take Francine to meet Edwin?'

Agnes shook her head. 'No, I don't think so. Zazz has offered to help me with the food so the two of us will see to that.' She glanced at Theo.

'Remember that envelope that Francine found with my name on it? I forgot to pick it up when we left. I should at least open it.'

'I popped it into the briefcase when I was up there. I'll bring it down in the next day or two. Not a problem.' Theo took a bite of his apricot tart, wondering whether now would be a good time to talk to Agnes about the file he'd hidden upstairs in his room. Knowing how upset she would be when he told her the news, he took the coward's way out and decided to leave it until after tonight's meeting with the Cortez's. And probably until next week. At least then Edwin would be here to help him give some moral support to whoever needed it.

Francine let herself into the cottage at lunchtime as usual. Theo had told her not to knock, to treat it like her own home and just walk in, so she did. There was a lovely vibe about this old cottage and she knew she would have been a lot happier staying down here with him and Agnes. Francine thought about Zazz staying on her own up in Oscar's house when everyone had returned to Devon after all this will business was settled. Would Zazz really be happy up there on her own? Somehow Francine doubted it. There were ghosts in the place even for Zazz she suspected. Maybe now Edwin was joining them this afternoon they could persuade her to change her mind and go home with them when they left.

Francine heard Agnes and Theo laughing together in the kitchen and she smiled to herself. Maman sounded so happy. Honestly, she and Theo were so good together she'd often wondered whether there could ever have been more between them. If only Maman had married Theo instead of Oscar all their lives would have been different and so much better, but she knew that union had always been out of the question. But now? Probably too late, sadly. Besides, if something had been going to happen between the two of them it would have happened years ago.

29

After Theo and Francine left for the airport Agnes found the iron and ironing board in the tall kitchen cupboard and set it up. She'd noticed that there was a small pile of clean washing on the machine waiting to be ironed. While Theo was out she planned on doing it for him. It was the least she could do.

Twenty minutes later Agnes carried the carefully folded shirts, jeans and towels up to Theo's bedroom and placed them on his bed. She'd leave them for him to put away, not wishing to open drawers and cupboards that were none of her business to see where he kept things.

Glancing around the room as she turned to leave she saw two silver framed photos on the bedside table. One was a group photo taken at Francine and Edwin's small intimate wedding. Bride and groom, groom's parents on his side, herself and Theo on Francine's side and one bridesmaid on both sides. Agnes walked across and picked up the photo, remembering what a perfect day it had been for the happy couple.

Francine had been adamant that she didn't want her father at the wedding and she'd asked Theo as her godfather and favourite uncle if he would walk her down the aisle. He'd been so proud that day to assume *in loco parentis* over Francine. Agnes remembered too how she'd stood at his side wishing that things could have turned out differently for her and Theo.

Carefully, Agnes replaced the photo before picking up the second one which was of herself. She smiled as she recognised the setting, the Royal Avenue Gardens in Dartmouth. Theo must have taken it on his phone during his last Christmas visit because she was standing by the town's Christmas tree admiring the decorations and pointing out something or other tied to its branches.

Returning the photo to its position on the bedside table, Agnes moved towards the door thinking about the one photo, also in a silver frame, she had on her own nightstand at home. Taken a few years ago now, she'd never replaced it with a more up to date one because she loved it so much. On one of his summer visits, the three of them had taken a river trip one evening on one of the tourist boats up to Totnes. Francine busy snapping photo after photo on her new phone had captured the two of them laughing at some joke or other. 'You look so happy in this photograph,' she said as she handed the printed version to Agnes. 'I thought you'd like a copy to keep. Show Theo.'

Agnes closed the bedroom door behind her and went downstairs, pushing all thoughts of what might have been so much more than a friendship, deep down inside her.

* * *

Zazz placed the last plate of food on the table and checked that everything was ready. 'Are you excited, Gran? I am. Can't wait to meet this new uncle of mine – well, half an uncle, and a half-cousin too.'

'I'm not sure that *excited* is the word,' Agnes said slowly.

'Curious yes but I'm more anxious than excited at the moment. I was hoping Theo and your parents would be here by now.'

'Plane was probably late landing and the traffic at this time of day is usually busy, especially on a Friday evening,' Zazz said. 'Don't worry, they'll be here soon. Besides aren't French people always a polite five minutes late? Which gives Theo a bit more time. Gran, can I ask you something? It's about Oscar so you probably won't want to answer,' Zazz said. 'Which is okay if you don't.'

Agnes glanced at her. 'I think it's time for honesty about the kind of man he was. Your mother and I made a mistake in not being more open with you about the past but it was easier to shut it away and not talk about him. What do you want to know?'

'I think he was a difficult, controlling man, from the little you've both said and patently someone I personally would hate to be married to so I sort of understand why you left him. But—'

'I ran away for my own safety,' Agnes interrupted quietly, giving her a serious look. 'Which is not something I've ever liked to talk about.'

'You mean he was violent towards you?'

Agnes gave a brief nod. '*Oui.*'

'You see, I didn't know that.'

'No reason for you to,' Agnes said. 'It didn't affect you, why did you need to know?'

'Was he violent towards Mum too?'

'I'm not sure.'

'So why did she cut contact with him as much as she could?'

Agnes sighed. 'Something happened on her last visit. She came back early, saying she hated him and never wanted to see him again but she wouldn't tell me why. I did ask if he'd assaulted her and she shook her head but something had clearly happened. Theo brought her home as he usually did but he was none the wiser either.'

'Does she know why you ran away in the beginning?'

'She was young, seven years old when it happened. I certainly wasn't going to tell her the truth at that point. It wasn't until she was old enough to visit Oscar on her own every summer that she started asking questions.' Agnes paused. 'And then I admit I gave her a toned-down account – a version *censurée* if you like, of why I had left her father. *Mais* since then, I tell her the truth.'

'Mum called him evil the other day,' Zazz said.

Agnes nodded. 'Evil is one word that describes him, immoral is another. The world is a better place now without Oscar Agistini in it, is all I can say.'

Zazz, hearing the tremble in her gran's voice quickly moved to her side and hugged her. 'Oh, Gran, I'm so sorry. I didn't mean to upset you.'

Agnes, taking a deep breath and visibly pulling herself together, gave a weak smile. 'It's easier not to speak of these things even now but I'm glad we've had this conversation.'

'So am I,' Zazz said. 'Thank you.'

'*Donc*! Time to get the *pissaladière* in the oven,' Agnes said. 'I always think it tastes better warm.' As she turned to go into the kitchen there was a bark at the front door. A second later it opened and Cerise rushed in, followed by everyone, and chaos reigned for several moments. Zazz quickly told her gran she'd see to the *pissaladière* and feed Cerise who had dashed through to the kitchen and was already sat by her food bowl waiting to be fed.

The two families had literally bumped into each other twenty metres from the front door and had quickly introduced themselves. Once indoors, Rachel took Serge across to introduce him to Agnes.

'My son, Serge,' she said.

'*Bonjour* Madame Agistini. *Enchanté*,' Serge said, shaking her hand as Agnes tried not to stare at him and keep her emotions under control. At first glance it could have been a young Oscar himself standing shaking her hand. Tall like his father, he'd inherited the Agistini Italian good looks but, like his newly acquired Uncle Theo, there was no harshness in his face, and his eyes twinkled with gentleness as he smiled at Agnes.

'Not a single doubt in my mind who your father was,' Agnes said softly. 'But I feel your maman was correct, you are not like him. You do not have his hardness of the eyes.'

'*Merci, madame*, I would not wish to be like him in any way,' Serge said, his Italian accent adding a delightful lyrical note to his spoken French. 'And thankfully my own son, Albert, shows no sign of inheriting any characteristics from the past.'

'That's good,' Agnes said, smiling.

Zazz, coming out of the kitchen with the warm *pissaladière*, faltered as she saw Albert standing next to Serge. Avoiding both his and Theo's surprised glance she quickly placed the plate on the table.

'Albert, would you give me a hand with fetching some water glasses from the kitchen *s'il vous plaît*?' And she disappeared back into the kitchen.

'Excuse me,' Albert said to Agnes and everyone. 'It seems my new cousin has need of my help,' and he followed Zazz into the kitchen.

'Push the door to. I can't believe it's you,' Zazz said. 'I have yet to tell my mother about the party where we met. She's going to be mad as hell with me when I tell her about it. If she asks you tonight where we met, could you just say we met briefly at a party somewhere in Cannes. Please don't mention it was at Oscar's. I need to tell her that particular bit of information myself.'

'Okay.'

'Thank you.' Zazz gave a sigh of relief. 'I have to ask – did you know you were Oscar's grandson that night?'

Albert shook his head. '*Non*. I wasn't sure why I was invited to be honest. Not my usual crowd to hang around with. Now, were you serious about water glasses?'

'Top shelf,' Zazz said, pointing. 'If you can manage half a dozen, I'll fill a jug with water.'

Back in the sitting room Theo had begun to hand glasses of champagne around and tentatively Agnes suggested a toast, '*Pour forger de nouveaux liens familiaux*. To family.'

Francine, sipping her champagne, regarded Serge and his mother over the rim of her glass. Rachel, a slim and quietly elegant woman whom Agnes had greeted with a kiss, was a million miles away from the woman Francine had imagined her to be. As for her newly acquired half-brother, he seemed to be a nice man. Not that you can always tell from first impressions of course, but she was prepared to try and get to know him. And Zazz was happily chatting away to Albert, her newly acquired cousin.

Once the initial awkwardness had worn off, talk turned to the serious business of Oscar's will.

'I will tell Monsieur Caumont that the affidavit Rachel signed is sufficient evidence that you are Oscar's son,' Agnes said. 'We do not need to double-check with DNAs. He only has to take a good look at you to see you're telling the truth.'

'Thank you,' Serge said.

'We need to clear the place before we can get it on the market. Do you want anything from the house? Have you ever been inside?'

Serge shook his head. '*Non*, I never go in the house and I have no need, except to maybe help you with moving things out?'

'I think we'll clear the personal things out and then get a

house clearance firm in. None of the furniture is particularly good,' Theo said, looking at Agnes for confirmation and she gave a nod.

'The other thing is – Oscar's ashes are currently here,' Agnes said. 'I do not wish to hold a memorial service but we do need to dispose of them. Do you want to be involved in any way? Hold your own service?'

Serge shook his head. '*Non*. I have zero respect for the man. I cannot be hypocritical and say otherwise. Do as you wish with them.' Serge looked at Agnes. 'I think I have the need to explain why I decided to claim my inheritance of Oscar's estate. I personally do not want the money. I do it for my maman, something to help her forget the pain Oscar inflicted on her.'

Agnes smiled at him. 'I understand completely. I am of the same mind.'

It was nearly eight o'clock when Zazz asked to be excused as she was meeting Mel and Dominic. 'It was great meeting you, Uncle Serge and Cousin Albert. I'm staying down for at least the next few months so maybe we can meet up again soon,' she said. As Zazz left, Rachel regretfully began to say they ought to think about leaving too and soon the party was over.

As Agnes stood in the doorway at Theo's side saying good-night to the Cortez's she sighed happily as she felt Theo's arm go around her shoulders. Unthinkingly, she leant into him.

It was good they'd managed to sort things out between themselves and the Cortez's without involving the notaire. First thing tomorrow morning she'd ring and make a rendez-vous with Monsieur Caumont and tell him about meeting with the Cortez's. He could go ahead with all the legal things then. Once the house was cleared and on the market, she could go home. Home. The thought made her catch her breath. In the short time she'd been back in the town of her birth she'd completely fallen in love with the place – it felt like home and was where she unexpectedly longed to live again. To spend the rest of her days in her true home. And to spend time with Theo.

She knew without him putting it into words, that it would make him so happy if she did stay on for a while. And he deserved to be happy. But was it the sensible thing for her to do after all these years? Shouldn't she simply accept the status quo and enjoy the loving friendship that had always existed between her and Theo? Rather than wishing for more.

30

Francine was waiting for Zazz in the kitchen when she returned from her run the next morning with the breakfast croissants. Zazz stifled a sigh. She knew what was coming. Leaving early last night hadn't given her mum a chance to interrogate her about Albert. Francine wasn't going to like the truth that was for sure.

'Morning, Mum. Croissants,' Zazz said brightly, holding them out to her mother. 'Where's Dad?'

'Thank you,' Francine said. 'Coffee,' and pushed a cup across the table to Zazz. 'Dad will be down in a moment.'

'I enjoyed the aperitifs last evening. The Cortez's seem nice. Agnes and Rachel get on well,' Zazz said.

'Agnes and Rachel were acquaintances when Granny lived here. I thought the same about you and Albert,' Francine said.

Zazz drank some coffee and replaced her cup on the table. 'I met him at a party the last time I was down here. People rarely introduce themselves properly at parties – he just said "Hi, I'm Al". No idea that was short for Albert or what his surname was and if he'd said, it wouldn't have meant anything to me at the time.'

'I presume the party was somewhere here in Cannes?' Francine said.

Zazz looked at her mum thoughtfully. This was the answer she wasn't going to like. 'Okay, full disclosure. I came over for Oscar's eighty-fourth birthday last year. He had a party here in the house – said he wanted to show off his granddaughter to his friends. Embarrassing or what? Especially as there were only about five people my age there, including Al – most were Oscar's age.'

'Was it a good party?' Francine stared at her. Zazz shrugged.

'It was okay but Oscar got very drunk. Al had barely intro-duced himself to me when Oscar dragged him away saying there was someone else he wanted him to meet.'

'Were you here in this house when you phoned me to wish me happy birthday?'

Zazz nodded. 'Yes. Up in my room.'

'So you lied about going to Ibiza with friends from work?'

'Well, I couldn't tell you where I was really going, could I? I've just had a thought,' Zazz looked at her mum. 'I suppose the fact that Al was at the party might mean that Oscar knew who he was. Al did say last night he didn't really know why he'd been invited. He definitely didn't know about Oscar's relationship to me until last evening.'

There was a silence before Francine spoke. 'I can't believe how you've behaved with this deception. You knew how Granny and I felt about Oscar and yet, and yet you deliberately went ahead to meet him and then planned to come and live with him.'

'Mum, whatever the problems have been for you and Granny with Oscar, it's all in the past. It wasn't my problem. If he hadn't died I possibly would have fallen out with him too in the future, but we'll never know now. I'm sorry I've hurt you and Granny but it was something I needed to do for me. I wanted to make up my own mind about him.'

'He phoned me on my birthday unexpectedly,' Francine said. 'Drunk as a skunk. To think you were in this house at the time. I couldn't understand a word he was saying. I hung up on him in the end. I knew there had to be a reason behind the phone call but couldn't work out what it was. Until now.' She pushed away her plate with the untouched croissant.

'I am certain that he wanted to gloat over me. I think the message he was too drunk to articulate to me that evening, was "you and your mother didn't want me but your daughter does".' Francine gave Zazz a sad look. 'And you giving him the opportunity to even think that, hurts.'

* * *

As they ate breakfast Francine suggested to Edwin that they spent the morning exploring Cannes.

'I can't wait to show you around.'

'Will Zazz come with us?'

'She's gone out already,' Francine said tight-lipped. 'We've fallen out again. Can you believe she lied to us about going to Ibiza. She came here for Oscar's last birthday.'

Edwin gave her a concerned look before he replied. 'I know it's hard but you have to accept Zazz needs to live her own life, decide who she wants in that life. I'm upset she came down behind our backs but I can understand why – look how cross you are after the event.'

'All these years of protecting her from Oscar pushed aside because she decided we had no right to keep them apart. Stupid, stupid girl.'

Edwin sighed. 'With hindsight, perhaps it would have been

better to have told her the reasons why you and Agnes wanted to keep her away from him. Shutting down the conversation every time she mentioned Oscar, refusing to talk about the man with her, clearly made her more curious.'

'At the time it felt the right thing to do. It just hurts that she appears to have taken his side against us by lying.'

'That's nonsense, she's not on anyone's side,' Edwin said. 'I think you're being too hard on Zazz. She never really got to know Oscar before he died. Now is the time to be honest with her. Tell her what you and Agnes went through. She doesn't have the knowledge you and Agnes have of Oscar's behaviour. Once you tell her she'll realise you, we, were trying to protect her.'

'I am so happy that Oscar died before Zazz moved in here with him. Terrible thing to say but,' Francine shrugged, 'I dread to think what could have happened.'

'The point is nothing had the chance to happen so you need to stop making it a bigger issue than it actually is now for Zazz.'

Francine stared at him but before she could say anything Edwin stood up.

'I think we need to finish this conversation and get some fresh air. Come on, let's get exploring. You promised to show me Cannes,' Edwin said, taking his coffee mug and plate over to the dishwasher. 'I need to walk along this wonderful Croisette I've heard so much about.'

Francine sighed. 'You're right. Come on then. First stop Allée des Étoiles du Cinema.' Edwin looked at her, his eyebrows raised. 'Wait and see.'

Twenty minutes later, having detoured to show Edwin the bustling Marché Forville, and passed several workmen struggling with hoardings to be put in place for the upcoming film festival, they were in front of the famous red steps of the Palais des Festivals. Walking with their eyes down they began looking at some of over three hundred handprints of famous stars embedded in the path known as the Allée des Étoiles.

'Cannes's answer to the Los Angeles Hollywood Walk of Fame. Look, Sophia Loren, Jean Paul Belmondo, Julie Andrews, Johnny Halliday, to name but a few. And here's Catherine Deneuve,' Francine said. 'Maman's favourite. I wonder if Theo has shown her this walkway yet.'

'I hadn't realised how fond Theo is of your maman,' Edwin said absently, wandering down the path towards her.

Francine glanced at him. 'What d'you mean?'

'Here in France they seem closer than they did on the occasions we've seen them together in Bath and Dartmouth, that's all. They seem to be more of a couple.'

'They've been in each other's lives a long time,' Francine said. 'They're comfortable with each other that's for sure. I know Maman was always waiting for Oscar to turn on Theo, which was something he'd done in the past apparently. Now that he's dead maybe they're both more relaxed?'

'That's probably it,' Edwin said, looking across at a gaily painted ice-cream stall. 'Fancy an ice-cream?'

'I was going to suggest stopping for a coffee but yes, a *glacé* instead would be lovely.'

* * *

Zazz, having decided she couldn't get out of the family dinner that evening, stayed close to her dad as the three of them left to walk down to meet Theo and Agnes on Saturday evening. Things were still strained between Francine and herself and she'd decided distance would be good. The restaurant Francine had booked was down on the busy Allées de la Liberté near the boules court. Zazz sank gratefully onto a chair between her dad and Theo.

Once they'd ordered their food – steaks for Edwin and Theo, *magret de canard* for Agnes and Francine and a vegetarian dish for Zazz, Edwin poured the wine. 'To think I've never been to the South of France before. I hope this is the first of many visits,' he said.

'You're welcome to come and visit me any time, Dad,' Zazz said. 'You too, Mum,' she added hurriedly, seeing the look on Francine's face.

'Thank you. We'll definitely be taking you up on that offer, won't we?' Edwin said, turning to Francine.

'Depends where Zazz will be living after the house is sold,' Francine said, glaring at Zazz. 'Studios don't generally have much room.'

Zazz sighed but didn't say anything, her mother had stated the truth. The apartment she and Mel were planning on sharing, although far bigger than a studio, didn't have a guest room.

'You're both more than welcome to stay with me any time,' Theo said.

'There you go, Mum, problem solved.'

Theo steered the conversation onto safer ground with his next remark. 'I was wondering about a visit to Saint Honorat tomorrow. The island is beautiful and the monastery there is well worth a visit and a Sunday morning I feel would be the perfect time. A visit there can really lift the spirits. It's a special place.'

'I'd like that,' Agnes said quietly. 'I remember going there years ago. Such a tranquil place.'

'It's Saint Marguerite that I remember more,' Francine said. 'Sailing over in the moonlight with friends, building a campfire on the beach and burnt sausages.' She laughed. 'I'm sure it was illegal but it was such fun. Next time I see Piers I must ask him if he remembers our illicit nighttime adventures. I'm sure he will.' She took a sip of her wine. 'Yes, let's do that tomorrow morning. A visit to the Îles d'Lérins after all these years will be good.'

Zazz, sitting there listening to her mother reminisce about her teenage holidays spent down here, wondered if Francine and Piers had ever been an item back in their teenage days. She quickly shut that thought down. Too weird to think about.

'I enjoyed meeting our new relatives last night,' Zazz said. 'My half-uncle seems okay and getting to know new cousin, Al, properly could be fun.' She smiled brightly at everyone before taking a sip of her wine.

'Are you being deliberately provocative?' Francine demanded.

'No. But like it or not they are part of our family. Our dysfunctional family.' Zazz turned to Agnes. 'You get on with Rachel, don't you, Gran?'

Agnes nodded. 'Yes. I think she had a hard start in life and what happened was all down to Oscar. He took advantage of a vulnerable young woman.'

'There you are then. Oscar guilty. Rachel innocent. We can all be friends.' Zazz knew that this time she was being provocative, but her mother was being downright impossible with her attitude.

Their meals arrived at that moment and to Zazz's relief conversation stilled for some time whilst everyone tucked into their food. As she ate her vegetarian enchiladas smothered with a spicy sauce that was delicious, she decided there was no way she was going on the boat trip tomorrow.

31

Zazz was relieved to find her dad on his own in the kitchen when she returned from her run early the next morning.

'Morning,' she said, putting the bag of croissants on the table as usual. 'Where's Mum?'

'Getting ready for our island trip. You'll have to be quick. We've got to leave in about fifteen minutes if we want to catch the first boat.'

'I'm not coming,' Zazz said as she popped a capsule into the coffee machine and pressed the button.

Edwin looked at her. 'Okay. That's a shame. I'm disappointed. I shall miss your company.'

'Sorry, Dad, but Mum and I are best staying away from each other at the moment.' She sighed. 'I seem to upset her every time I open my mouth or give her an honest answer to a question.'

'You did provoke her a little last night though, whether it was deliberate or not,' Edwin said.

'It was and it wasn't deliberate. I just thought mentioning the Cortez's rather than shying away from talking about them would be a good thing. I should have known better. I'll take my croissant and coffee upstairs out of the way. Have a lovely time – maybe we can go again together another day?'

'Definitely. You have a good day.'

Zazz stayed up in her room until she heard the front door slam and her parents leaving. She'd half expected Francine to come up and argue with her about not going with them, but she didn't and Zazz suspected her dad had told her not to. Shower time. Afterwards she would take a walk around the artisan market Mel had told her about.

Marché Forville was busy as she walked through, dodging around people, soaking up the atmosphere as she took photo after photo. Marcus might like a feature about the history of the market, particularly as it had recently been refurbished. One photo she took made her smile. An elderly man was carefully choosing *salade* items from one of the legumes stalls with a large ginger cat, complete with collar and lead, contentedly curled around his shoulders, the cat's blue eyes watching every movement of the stall holder.

When she reached the brocante and artisan open air market held on Les Allées de la Liberté, Zazz stood on the edge of the open space and took several photos from a distance, trying to capture the size of the event. So many stalls – second-hand books, china, vinyl records, postcards, toys, furniture, pictures, jewellery. In amongst the second-hand stalls were stands selling new screen-printed scarves, paintings, old-fashioned wooden toys, an author selling his latest book, straw baskets, handmade jackets and hats. The market offered a real cornucopia of goods to buy, new and old – and lots of good content for her blog and photos for Instagram.

Zazz wandered around looking at everything, trying to resist the urge to buy a straw sun hat she fell in love with and failing. She was in the South of France, sun protection was a must.

Thought about like that the hat was an investment and a must-have.

Desperate for a coffee, after paying for her hat she decided she was all marketed-out and made her way to Piers's cafe. Unusually, there was a long queue outside and she could see a harassed Dominic and Piers busy inside.

'*Excusez-moi*,' she said pushing through the queue. '*Je travaille ici.*'

Piers saw her coming and smiled. 'You come to assist?'

Zazz nodded. 'Looks like you need a hand.' She looked across at the sink filled with coffee cups waiting to go in the dishwasher. 'Shall I start there?'

Piers nodded. 'Thanks.' And he turned back to the queue. The next hour passed in a blur as Zazz caught up with the dirty crockery before clearing and wiping tables and generally keeping on top of things.

'*Merci beaucoup*,' Piers said as the queue finally dwindled away. 'A Sunday morning *exceptionel*. Andre asked for the day off and I did not think we'd be so busy. The festival doesn't begin until Wednesday, when it will be like this every day, but then I have extra staff and Mel helps.'

'I'm happy to help too if you're desperate again,' Zazz said. 'Reminds me of working in cafes when I was a student.' She smiled as Dominic handed her a cup of coffee. 'Thanks.'

'Supper tonight as a thank you from me?' Dominic said quietly as Piers moved away to serve a customer. Zazz hesitated.

'I think you are going to say it's not necessary but it's just an excuse for me to ask you out again. So please, have supper with me tonight?'

Zazz smiled at him. '*Merci*. That would be lovely.'

* * *

'It was supposed to be a family outing,' Francine said when Edwin told her Zazz wasn't coming with them to Saint Honorat. 'I suppose she blames me.'

'Not directly, no,' Edwin said diplomatically. 'She just feels that every time she says something she upsets you. She didn't want to spoil the day. There will be other family outings. Right. Are we ready for this boat trip?'

Francine nodded. 'Yes. It's a lovely day so hopefully the sea will be calm.'

As the four of them walked along the quay towards the tourist boats at the far end, Francine pointed out Piers's boat to Edwin. 'He was always sailing mad. I'm pleased he's done well and has his dream yacht.'

The tourist boat was crowded but they managed to find seats on the outside deck and were soon travelling across the bay to the Îles de Lérins. Francine sniffed the sea breeze and enjoyed feeling the occasional spray as the boat cut through the water. Fifteen minutes later the boat was skilfully manoeuvred alongside the landing stage and people started to disembark.

'If we walk along this path,' Theo said, pointing. 'We should be in time to catch Mass in the Abbey. Only if you want to, of course. The doors are closed while the Mass is happening and no-one can leave during the celebration. Afterwards you can wander in at will for a private moment. You can hear the chanting from outside a little.'

'I'd like to be in the church for the chanting,' Agnes said quietly. 'It's so long since I heard the monks chant.'

'I'm happy to do that with you,' Theo said.

'I'd rather wander in later for a private moment,' Francine said.

'I'd prefer to do that too,' Edwin agreed.

The four of them walked along the path Theo had indicated

and were soon standing by the pathway leading into the Abbey. Clumps of lavender that would perfume the way later in the year were interspersed with shrubs and bougainvillaea that bordered the path. Signs with the single word 'SILENCE' written on them were dotted at intervals down the length of the long path.

'We're in time for Mass,' Theo whispered. 'Catch up with you two by the boutique in about an hour?' And he and Agnes began to walk down the path towards the open door of the Abbey.

Feeling intimidated by the silence signs Francine looked at Edwin, caught hold of his hand and pulled him in the direction they should go. Once they were away from the demanded silence near the Abbey she relaxed. 'Come on, let's walk and soak up the atmosphere of the place. And I'll try and remember what I know about the history of the island.'

'I know there have been Cistercian monks living on the island since 410. I think they follow the rule of Saint Benedict. The vineyard is small, about eight hectares but the wines and the liqueurs they produce are world famous.'

By the time they'd explored several small coves, roamed down paths lined with olive trees and Aleppo pines, gazed at the hectares of vines being tended by monks in their white robes, Edwin too had fallen under the spell of the island.

Agnes and Theo were waiting for them when they reached the cluster of boutiques by the restaurant.

'We were wondering about lunch in the restaurant,' Agnes said. 'It has a very good reputation.'

'Why don't we buy some food from the snack bar over there and have a picnic?' Francine said. 'I still feel full after last night's lovely meal. There are some picnic tables not far away.'

'Good idea,' Theo said. 'Pan Bagnats all round? A bottle of rosé between us?'

Francine pointed out the direction to Edwin where she

remembered seeing picnic tables a few metres away hidden by the pine trees. 'We'll go and bag a table,' and she and Agnes left the men to buy the food.

Sitting there, looking across the Bay of Cannes towards the mainland, Agnes sighed happily. 'It feels so good to be back,' she said, glancing at Francine. 'Are you happy to be back down here?'

'Yes. I'm starting to feel as though I've never been away. Edwin and I will certainly visit now whenever we can. You can come with us.'

'I can, can't I?' Agnes said thoughtfully.

'When the house is sold we could use our share to buy a lock-up-and-leave apartment? I'm sure Theo would keep an eye on it for us. We could all come down then whenever we wanted.'

'Theo has already offered us his cottage to stay in as often as we want to,' Agnes said.

Francine nodded. 'I know but I wouldn't want to take advantage. It's good to be independent. Here's lunch,' she said as Theo and Edwin appeared.

The size of small plates, the Pan Bagnats were stuffed full of salad, egg and tuna and were, everybody agreed, quite delicious.

Edwin, gazing out over the Mediterranean towards the mainland coastline, shook his head in wonder. 'This place is so beautiful, so tranquil, it's hard to remember that over there, a short distance away, the twenty-first century is in full swing with all its attendant commercialism.'

Theo gave a sad smile. 'I agree. Life today is fast and furious compared to life here on the island for the monks. But even here the monks have to run a commercial business in order to survive and maintain the ancient Abbey as well as their slower, chosen, way of life.'

Agnes brushed the crumbs off her lap and stood up. 'And I, for one, am grateful to the monks for providing us with an idyllic escape from the real world – and making such delicious wine and liqueurs. Two bottles of which are waiting for Theo to collect from the boutique.'

* * *

Zazz wasn't sure what to wear for her supper date with Dominic. She hadn't brought many date-wearing clothes with her – mainly jeans and tops. In the end she decided on her favourite posh white jeans, a long-sleeved Breton-style top with red stripes, teamed with her denim waistcoat in case the evening turned chilly, and she slipped her feet into her wedge sandals. Dominic had invited her for supper not dinner so hopefully they would go to a bistro-type place rather than a posh restaurant.

Dominic had said he'd come up to Le Suquet for her and they could walk down together but Zazz had quickly suggested they met in town and had persuaded Dominic to meet her at the bottom of rue Saint Antoine. Introducing him to her parents, her mother in particular, wasn't going to happen tonight. He was waiting for her and greeted her with a kiss on the cheek.

'I hope you like pasta,' he said, looking at her. 'Because we're going to the best pasta bistro in Cannes.'

'Love pasta,' Zazz said.

'Good. Come on then, it's five minutes down this way.'

Dominic pushed open a nondescript door and revealed a spacious courtyard with several huge terracotta pots containing olive trees or oleander plants dotted around, a rampant bougainvillaea covered its stone walls and at the far end a loggia was covered with the blue flowers of plumbago. Tables and chairs were placed under the loggia and also higgledy-piggledy around the courtyard amongst the plants. Fairy lights were entwined in amongst all the greenery and solar lights in the pots were starting to shine as dusk fell.

Zazz looked around her in amazement. 'What a wonderful place. It's magical.' She kept the words 'and romantic' to herself.

'One of Cannes's best-kept secrets,' Dominic said. 'If you don't know about it you'll never find it. The food's good too.'

A waiter came forward, obviously a friend as he laughed and greeted Dominic by name before showing them to a table for two under the loggia. There was a large window on the back wall and Zazz watched, fascinated, as the team of chefs and sous-chefs danced around each other in the kitchen as they all concentrated on stirring and shaking pans, intent on producing the best food for their customers. It was like watching a ballet without music. Zazz guessed there must be noise in the kitchen but none could be heard in the courtyard.

She took Dominic's advice and chose the linguine with French green beans, parsley pesto and freshly grated pecorino Romano cheese, The fresh Sauvignon Blanc wine with its herb overtones he chose to accompany their meal was perfect too.

As they ate, Dominic talked a little about various films he'd seen and Zazz quickly realised he was a bit of a film buff. She hadn't heard of half the films he mentioned – just the blockbuster ones. He laughed when she confessed to loving anything with George Clooney and Julia Roberts in.

When he asked if there was a boyfriend back in the UK, she shook her head and told him about Rufus. Dominic mentioned being hurt too by a previous relationship but didn't go into details, simply saying it was a few years ago now.

'Do you like working with your papa in the coffee shop?' she asked. Dominic nodded.

'I love it. Can't wait to take it over when Papa retires like he keeps threatening to do.' Andre, his younger brother, wasn't interested in being involved in the business full time and had plans to go to America once he'd graduated. 'His ambition is to work for a year or two in California and then he wants to return to Sophia Antipolis, the Riviera's answer to Silicon Valley, and set up his own high-tech company here.' Dominic shuddered. 'I can't think of anything worse than sitting behind a computer all day.'

Zazz talked about concentrating on her social media business and about wanting to write a novel one day. She'd never told anyone else that, and was surprised she felt so comfortable telling Dominic and was glad he didn't rubbish her dream.

They shared a huge tiramisu for dessert and enjoyed small coffees afterwards, although Dominic pulled a face at the coffee. 'Not as good as ours,' he whispered.

After supper he took her hand as they walked along the Croisette looking at the lights, the big glitzy 'Welcome to Cannes' sign hanging over the Croisette ready for the festival, coloured lights wound around the palm tree trunks, more lights strung between the trees.

As they passed the Palais des Festivals Dominic said, 'I have two tickets for the second Thursday evening film screening, not sure the film will be to your liking – George Clooney isn't in it – but would you like to come and brave the red carpet with me?'

'Seriously? I'd love to,' Zazz said.

'Great.'

Dominic insisted on walking her home. At the door she turned and said, 'Thank you for a lovely evening.'

'The first of many I hope,' Dominic said before placing a fleeting kiss on her cheek and leaving. 'See you soon.'

Once up in her room she sent Mel a text.

> See you as usual in the morning? I need your help.

32

Mel was waiting for Zazz on the quay early the next morning, a big smile on her face. 'Who had supper with my big brother then? What kind of help are you after?'

'I'll tell you as we run,' Zazz said. 'Dominic has asked me to go to a screening at the Palais des Festivals during the film festival. I've said yes of course but what do I wear? Please point me in the right direction.'

'No problem. I'll take you to a few of my favourite boutiques and help you choose something spectacular to walk up the red carpet and those famous steps.' Mel glanced at her. 'Dominic gets tickets every year but has never taken a girlfriend before. He must like you a lot. How about you? Do you like him?'

'You're not going to become the protective sister, are you?' Zazz said. 'I do like him but I've only just come out of a relationship so I'm not looking for anything serious right now. And I also need to concentrate on my new career. I did tell Dom that last evening. He seemed fine with us being friends.'

'Friends with benefits?'

Zazz shrugged. 'Maybe in the future. Right now we're getting to know each other. We've only just met, Mel, but I do like him – despite him being your brother,' she said, laughing at the expression on Mel's face at her words.

After their run, Zazz collected the usual bag of breakfast croissants from her favourite boulangerie. Once back at the house she left the bag on the kitchen table and ran upstairs to take a shower before joining her parents for breakfast in the kitchen.

Her phone pinged with an e-mail from Marcus. 'Yes,' she said, punching the air with delight as she read it.

'Marcus is going to give my blog and my YouTube channel a mention in the magazine.'

'Well done,' Edwin said. 'Look forward to seeing your name in the magazine and boasting about my daughter, the influencer. Think we might open a bottle of bubbly tonight to celebrate.'

'Thanks, Dad.' Zazz looked at her mother questioningly. 'Mum? Aren't you pleased for me? The magazine has a huge circulation online.'

'Yes, of course I am. Huge congratulations,' Francine said.

'You don't sound terribly convincing. I sense a but?'

'It's just I worry about you being so far away from home trying to create a new life for yourself in a strange country. As for living here in this house on your own initially, I do worry,' Francine shook her head. 'I know you've been living independently ever since Dad and I left but Bath is a lot closer to Devon than Cannes is, should you need anything.'

'Have you forgotten that thanks to you and Gran I'm half French? It's not a totally strange country. Great-Uncle Theo is only down the road. I'm sure he'd be the first to help me if I ever needed it,' Zazz said. 'And as for living in this house, Mel wants me to share an apartment with her after September, so I won't be totally on my own for long in any case.'

'Well, that's something,' Francine said. 'Dad's right, we'll celebrate your magazine success tonight with a bottle of bubbly. Are
you free to give us a hand today? We really need to start clearing
things out ready for the place to go on the market.'

'Sure. I can help this morning but this afternoon I need to do
some content planning and update all three of my social media
channels. What do you want to do first?'

'Pack up all Oscar's clothes ready for Sunny Bank, the local
charity.'

'I can do that if you like,' Edwin offered. 'I know it's not a job
you are looking forward to.'

'Thanks,' Francine said. 'In that case, Zazz, you and I can
make a start on cleaning the unused bedroom.'

33

Monday evening and knowing Agnes and he had a rendez-vous with the notaire the next day, Theo decided time had run out and he couldn't keep quiet about the folder any longer. He had to show Agnes all the incriminating paperwork and tell her what Oscar had done. If Agnes agreed they would take the file with them and show it to the notaire. It was doubtful that he could do anything about it after all this time but Theo was of the opinion he still needed to be told.

Agnes was sitting out in the courtyard happily reading and looked up when Theo fetched the briefcase from his room and placed it on the small courtyard table. She looked up in surprise.

'I need to talk to you. Here's the envelope with your name on it,' he said taking it out of the briefcase and handing it to her.

'Thank you,' Agnes said barely glancing at it before laying it on the table and regarding Theo curiously.

'You know I've sorted out Oscar's papers. Everything was in order and correct until I found this.' He pushed the folder across the table towards her. 'I wish I didn't have to show you this but,' he shrugged, 'everything looks to have been drawn up legally when looked at initially but it most definitely isn't when you know the truth.'

'The truth about what? Theo, you are worrying me now,' Agnes said, putting her book down on top of the envelope. 'Whatever is it? Has Oscar murdered someone and hidden the evidence? I wouldn't put it past him.'

'No but he has committed a crime that affects you. It was the name on the folder that first drew my attention,' Theo said, pointing to it.

Agnes looked closely at the file for the first time. 'Denice Bernard? My sister, Denice? She'd left home before I met him. How could Oscar even know my sister?' Agnes looked at him uncertainly.

Theo gave a quick shrug. 'I don't know. Maybe the notaires put them in touch. Or perhaps she came home for a visit and your parents introduced them without telling you?'

Agnes shook her head. 'I wouldn't know. I never heard from my parents again after I left here with Francine. Oscar rang and told me first about Maman dying, and then Papa two years later. On both occasions he said as he was still my legal husband, he'd take charge and deal with everything. If there was anything due to me he'd make sure I got it. I must admit I didn't really welcome his involvement. I wanted to contact the notaire myself. I certainly didn't inherit anything from either of them.'

'Agnes, you need to think about this carefully. Did you have any correspondence sent to you from notaires about your parents when they died? About your inheritance?'

'No. I told you, Oscar insisted on handling everything for me, so all the paperwork must have gone to him. Even if there wasn't much actual money after Papa died the house would have been sold. I figured they'd found a way of cutting me out of the will after all when I didn't receive anything.'

Theo took a deep breath. 'You know French law doesn't work like that. It was impossible for them to cut you out and they didn't. But Oscar did.'

'What?'

'You and Denice each inherited fifty thousand euros when the house was sold after your papa died.' Theo took a deep breath. 'Oscar kept all of your share.' Theo looked at her. 'I'm so sorry.'

Agnes looked at him, stunned. 'But how could he do that? Surely Monsieur Caumont knew about me. And wouldn't there have been papers to sign?'

'He used a different notaire, not Monsieur Caumont. Someone from Marseille. As for papers to be signed, he forged your signature whenever he had to. He would have also lied about where you were. I'm guessing too, that's why he refused to divorce you when you mentioned a no-fault divorce a few years ago.'

Theo rifled through some of the papers. 'There's also a letter here from Denice who was living in Paris at the time your papa died, asking about you and where exactly you were. For some reason Oscar kept a carbon copy of the letter from him to Denice explaining why it was impossible for her to come and see you but he'd continue to pass on any messages that she'd like to give him.' He held up a piece of flimsy A4 paper. 'It's a bit smudged after all these years but it's still readable. You apparently were ill and not well enough to receive visitors.'

'Oscar certainly didn't pass on any of her messages to me. I've never heard a word from Denice since the day she left home.'

Agnes looked at him as she fought back tears. 'I would have loved to have had my sister back in my life years ago. I missed her more than my parents if I'm truthful.'

'I know,' Theo said sadly. 'I think tomorrow we have to show these papers to the notaire. Sadly, I suspect there is nothing he can do at this late stage, especially as Oscar is dead.'

Agnes looked at the file on the table. 'Oscar was such a devious man. I've always hated him and I didn't think it was possible to hate him any more than I have done for years now that he is dead, but keeping my sister away from me.' She closed her eyes and took a deep breath. 'I am so, so, glad he is dead and can't hurt me any more.'

'I did find something in the file that I think you'll like,' Theo said.

Agnes opened her eyes and looked at him.

'Denice's address and telephone number.'

'Really? Her address in Paris?'

'She lives in Juan-les-Pins now.'

'Denice is back living down here? I always believed she'd stay in Paris. There's a phone number as well? Will you ring her? Take me to see her?'

'*Oui*, there is a phone number. And *bien sûr* we will go together.'

'Would you ring her soon and ask if you can go and see her? Perhaps after the notaire's visit tomorrow. Make some excuse or other but don't tell her about me. I want it to be a surprise,' Agnes said.

'I'll phone her in the morning,' Theo said. 'Before we go to the notaire.'

'I'm so excited. Shall we keep this news to ourselves until I've met up with her again?' Agnes said. 'I hope she will be as pleased as I am to be in touch again. Growing up we were so close. I was devastated when she left. I can't believe over half a century after she left my sister is living back down on the Riviera and I'm going to see her again.'

Later that evening in her bedroom getting ready for bed,

Agnes's thoughts kept returning to Denice. She remembered Denice being the best big sister ever. Always protective of her and great fun. The two of them had shared a bedroom and as Agnes grew up and became a teenager, Denice, two years older, began to treat her as her best friend and, once she'd sworn her to secrecy, had started to confide her innermost dreams to her.

Agnes had always known how much she longed to be an actress, maybe even go to Hollywood and star in films. Denice loved the film festival, hanging around the Palais des Festivals, haunting the coffee shops where the stars went, begging for autographs as they walked along the Croisette. In those long-ago days there had been very little security. Denice claimed to have had a conversation with Kirk Douglas one morning, and on another day had sat next to Brigitte Bardot on the sand.

How she was going to run away one day because their parents wouldn't let her live the life she wanted to, became her main topic of conversation. Their parents didn't take her threats seriously though, her mother simply pleading with her to grow up, her father threatening dire consequences. And then one day, Denice simply left. No note, no goodbye to Agnes. Just gone out of their lives.

Agnes had been as shocked as anyone. Denice had always maintained she wasn't going to tell her the exact date when she planned to leave or where she was going, saying it was better if she didn't know details – she'd be able to tell the truth then, when asked what she knew. Nothing. 'You can't lie to save your life,' she'd said, smiling at her.

Agnes remembered the horrible days and weeks immediately after Denice had left. Her mother was distraught, her father angry. One particular memory stood out. Denice had left some of her clothes and Agnes had daringly tried on a mini dress. Shorter than Denice by a couple of inches, the dress had covered her knees rather than barely covering her thighs like it had on her sister. But it fitted her body and she felt good in it. All was well until her father saw her wearing it and yelled at her to take it off instantly. She was not to wear anything of Denice's ever again. And to make sure, her father instructed her mother to throw away everything Denice had left behind. Agnes managed to secrete away a navy silk scarf with scarlet Eiffel Tower motifs over it and wore it when her father was absent.

She smiled to herself. That scarf, like her Celtic pendant, had been one of the things that Agnes had hidden away but could always lay her hands on. She hadn't brought the scarf with her to France but she knew exactly where it was back home in Devon. She looked forward to reuniting Denice with it one day.

34

'After all our hard work today I think we deserve some fresh air and maybe a glass of wine at one of the bars?' Edwin said as he and Francine closed the last box full of stuff to go to Sunny Bank.

'Definitely,' Francine agreed. 'A walk along the quay would be great. Some sea air to blow the cobwebs away. Maybe Piers will be on his boat and I can finally introduce the two of you.'

Piers's boat was all closed up and there was no sign of him as the two of them walked past. 'Another time,' Francine said. 'Going for a coffee in his cafe might be better.' They walked on further until they were level with the big hotel on the bend of the coast road.

'Shall we have a glass of wine in their bar?' Edwin said. 'Or would you prefer somewhere else?'

'It looks a bit intimidating,' Francine said. 'I don't really feel dressy enough for a place like that. Let's wander back. There's a small place in the square near the steps by Theo's cottage.' They retraced their steps but this time as they passed Piers's boat he was on board and smiled in welcome as he saw them. Francine introduced the two men and Piers insisted they stepped on board for a glass of wine.

'Zazz, she helped us out in the cafe yesterday morning. We were so grateful. My son, Dominic, took her for supper last night in his favourite Italian bistro to say thank you.'

'The same son who took her to the cinema the other evening?' Francine said. 'She didn't mention it to us.' She glanced at Edwin, who simply shrugged his shoulders.

'No rule that she has to tell us her every movement,' he said. 'She's been independent now for some time and once we return to Devon, we'll have no idea of what she's up to down here.'

'With my boys I am much more relaxed about their social life whereas with Mel, I have to stop myself from being too inquisitive,' Piers smiled. 'Perhaps it is something to do with a father's protection towards a daughter.'

'Maybe,' Francine said. 'Although I don't recall Oscar being overly blessed in that direction towards me. It was always Mum and Theo looking out for me.'

'Frankie, you had friends looking out for you down here,' Piers said quietly. 'I remember Theo telling me to take care of you because...' He hesitated. 'Because of your difficult home life.'

'I didn't realise that,' Francine said. 'Belated thanks,' and she smiled at him.

'It was always a pleasure to see you every summer,' Piers said.

'We were over on Saint Honorat yesterday and I was telling Edwin about our nighttime camp fires on the beach on Saint Marguerite beach.'

'Ah, the good old days. Impossible to do that now, too many rules and regulations,' Piers said.

'Kids today don't know what they're missing,' Francine said, finishing her wine and glancing at Edwin. 'I think we'd better make a move. We've got more house clearing to face tomorrow and I think an early night would be a good idea.'

They were walking back up to Oscar's, when Edwin said. 'How well did you really know Piers in the past? He seems very fond of you still all these years later. Calling you Frankie is not something I've ever dared to call you in all the time I've known you.'

'It's what all my friends down here called me. I guess it was a teenage name that I outgrew.' Francine glanced at Edwin, surprised. 'You're not jealous, are you?'

'No. Just interested.'

'Piers and I were close but we were never a couple in that we slept together. I think if I hadn't left like I did, then maybe something would have happened between us that summer, I honestly don't know. I always looked forward to seeing him but I hadn't thought about him in years. It was quite a surprise meeting up with him.' Francine shrugged. 'Now he thinks I'm an uptight English woman. Very different to the "spontaneous" girl he knew all those years ago. I know you think I'm too hard on Zazz,' Francine said. 'Does that mean you agree with Piers that I'm uptight?'

When Edwin didn't answer straight away she stopped and looked at him. 'I'll take your silence as a yes then.'

Edwin took hold of her hand. 'I think you get uptight over things you cannot control because you care. Zazz is a good kid, she's grown into a lovely young woman and now she has to find her own way in life. You can't keep protecting her. As for not being spontaneous, well work and responsibilities tend to take precedence over spontaneity for us all. But,' Edwin squeezed her hand, 'we are coming to the time of our lives when we can decide how busy we want to be and make time for ourselves. I think we can practise doing things together on the spur of the moment. I don't remember you ever being particularly spontaneous but I do remember you being fun. Maybe you need to try and re-kindle your inner Frankie?'

The rest of the walk home continued in silence. As they closed the front door behind them Francine turned to Edwin.

'I fancy a soak in the bath tonight rather than having a shower.'

'While you go ahead and soak, I'll check my e-mails. I'm expecting one that might mean I have to go home sooner than I planned.' Edwin went through to the kitchen as Francine made for the stairs.

'Give me a shout if you want me to scrub your back, Frankie,' Edwin called out.

Francine turned and stared after him before going upstairs and into the bathroom. Like that was going to happen. Of course she didn't want him to scrub her back. That would only lead to them having sex and after that uptight remark she wasn't in the mood. She turned on the taps and once hot water was gushing into the bath poured in an extravagant amount of bath oil and soon the perfume of her favourite rose-scented bath oil began to fill the bathroom air.

Checking that her towel was on the rail, she stripped off, leaving her clothes on the floor and stepped into the bath. She lay back and closed her eyes, letting the hot water sooth and relax her body as she tried to empty her mind. Bliss. But it wasn't long before niggling thoughts began to creep back in. She'd always thought of herself as level-headed, in control, calm in a crisis and generally capable of dealing with anything life chose to throw at her. Uptight though? Did that really describe her these days? She was beginning to suspect it did.

Had she really changed that much since Piers had known her all those years ago? Why hadn't she noticed that she'd become this uptight person? When had she lost her French *la joie de vivre* as Piers had put it so succinctly? "An uptight English woman" he'd called her. It couldn't just be to do with the fact that after the age of seven she'd grown up in England. She and Agnes talked French all the time and Agnes had made sure she knew all about her hometown Cannes, the place of her birth, as well as the history of France. True, there hadn't been talk of any family relations, no visits from grandparents or aunts, just Uncle Theo. But there had been those six teenage fortnights of annual holiday spent here in this very house. Holidays that had shown her a whole different way of living, one that she had assumed she would always have access to.

Memories of the way that last holiday had suddenly ended flashed into her mind. Arriving back in Devon with Uncle Theo, determined not to let her maman know how upset she was about the opportunity she'd had to refuse. She remembered too, being equally determined to be in control of her own life when she turned eighteen a week or two later. Her father had had his last opportunity to be involved in her life. From then on she was going to apply careful thought to which direction would be the best for her to go in.

Was that the beginning of her losing her spontaneity? Of becoming uptight? Edwin said he didn't remember her being spontaneous but she had been fun to be with when they first met. Clearly she wasn't fun these days.

Thoughtfully, Francine stretched out a leg and turned the hot tap on with her foot. Things were so different these days. So many different opportunities where anything seemed to be attainable to Zazz's generation. Zazz. Francine sighed. She loved Zazz so much but would have to admit she hadn't been the best mother to her in recent months. Zazz, asserting her independence by deciding to stay in Bath and not move with them when

Francine and Edwin left for Dartmouth, had been something of a shock.

In a lightbulb moment as she reached for the soap, Francine realised it had been empty nest syndrome in reverse. The child staying and the mother leaving. So, when they were together, she'd tried too hard to convince herself that Zazz still needed her in her life but had only succeeded in driving a wedge between them. At least now she realised the problem she could start to mend their relationship.

Now all she had to do was find her inner 'Frankie'. Maybe she could start tonight. 'Edwin,' she called. 'I think maybe I do need you to scrub my back.'

35

Theo rang Denice in the morning before leaving for the notaire's office as he'd promised but was connected to a messaging service. He left his name and telephone number and asked Denice to ring him as soon as possible. There was no reply before they had to leave for the notaire's.

'*Bonjour*,' Monsieur Caumont said as he ushered Agnes and Theo into his office. 'You have brought me some papers?' he asked, looking at the file Theo was holding.

'Something we feel you should know about but in reality we think it's too late to rectify,' Theo said.

'But first,' Agnes said, 'I have decided about the DNA tests. I do not think they are necessary. Rachel Cortez has signed a legal document knowing the consequences if she lies. I have now met both Rachel and Serge and also Serge's son and accept that Serge is the illegitimate son of Oscar.'

The notaire sighed. 'It is irregular but I can only advise in this case.'

'You have met him, surely you recognise the family likeness,' Agnes said.

Monsieur Caumont nodded. '*Oui. D'accord.* We will proceed on the basis of the legal quarter for you and a two-way split of the remainder between the children of Oscar Agistini – Madame Mansell and Monsieur Cortez. Do you, Madame Agistini, intend to live in the house?'

'Definitely not,' Agnes said.

'The house will need to be sold then. Would you like my property manager to deal with that?'

'Please.'

'It would be good if we could get it on the market whilst the film festival is running,' the notaire said thoughtfully. 'It is not a Belle Epoque villa but its situation in Le Suquet makes it a desirable property and there will be a lot of creative people in town who would love to get their hands on such a house. *Bon.* I will ask my property manager, Suzette, to call you urgently and make arrangements for a visit and to take photographs. Perhaps we can even hold an "Open Viewing" morning.' He looked at the file in Theo's hands.

Theo took a deep breath and handed it to him. 'I found it going through Oscar's papers. It would appear that he swindled Agnes out of her parents' inheritance.'

'Oh, come Monsieur Agistini, that is extremely unlikely,' the notaire protested. 'There are regulations in place to prevent such a happening. I think perhaps you misunderstand. I will have a quick look and set your mind at rest. Would you like a coffee while I read through?' When Agnes and Theo both said please, he pressed a button on his desk. '*Trois cafés, s'il vous plaît.*'

Drinking her coffee, Agnes tried to read the notaire's expression but apart from the occasional twitch of his mouth he remained poker faced. Ten long minutes passed with Agnes and Theo watching and waiting. Finally Monsieur Caumont closed the file with a deep sigh.

'My apologies, Monsieur Agistini, you were right. Your brother did indeed swindle his wife out of her inheritance.' He looked Agnes. 'The notaire he used in Marseille was struck off ten years ago for seriously dishonest conduct and has since died. I can report it and have this case added to his record but...' He shook his head.

'There's little point, is there?' Agnes said quietly. 'The money has gone.'

The notaire shook his head. 'Yes. I am so sorry.'

'Apropos of absolutely nothing,' Theo asked quietly. 'Are you aware that my brother had a fifty-foot motor yacht?'

'I know nothing about any boat.' The notaire looked at Theo, surprised. 'It's not mentioned in his papers.'

'That's good, because my brother verbally promised it to me in the event of his death.' Theo held Monsieur Caumont's gaze. 'I intend to sell it.'

The notaire gave Theo a slow enigmatic smile and nodded, before shaking Theo's hand. 'I think that is a good way to proceed. But we've never had this conversation.'

'Thank you,' Theo said, returning his smile and picking up the folder.

Walking back to Theo's cottage Agnes said, 'Did Oscar really promise to leave the boat to you?'

'*Non.*' Theo turned to look at her. 'D'you know how much Oscar's boat turns out to be worth?'

'No idea,' Agnes said. 'I've never had much interest in boats.'

'Somewhere in the region of forty-five thousand euros, possibly more. Which, with a little bit of luck, should be in your bank account some time in the near future when the boat is sold.'

Agnes stopped dead. 'How much? Shouldn't it be included as part of Oscar's estate and be divided between Francine and Serge?'

'It's not listed amongst Oscar's assets. The notaire knows nothing about a boat. Once it's sold the proceeds will go some way to repaying you the money Oscar swindled you out of – and probably used to buy the boat in the first place.'

'And the notaire is happy with you doing this?'

'Like he said, we've never had a conversation about it!'

Agnes smiled at him, before leaning in and kissing his cheek. 'Thank you.'

* * *

Edwin and Francine joined them that evening, bringing boxes of takeaway pizzas for supper, after spending the day clearing, cleaning and tidying things up at Oscar's.

'This morning at the notaire's we put the house on the market with him and he's sending someone round to take photographs and measurements soon,' Agnes said. 'He seems to think it will sell quite quickly. He's talking about holding an "open viewing" morning if there is enough interest, probably during the last week of the festival.'

'That sounds like a good idea,' Edwin said. 'That kind of thing often results in a quick sale.'

'We've decided to treat ourselves to a day out tomorrow,' Francine said. 'Take the train along the coast and explore Monaco. Would you two like to come with us? We asked Zazz if she wanted to come but she's going shopping with Mel to buy a dress to wear for her red-carpet adventure with Dominic.'

'Cannes was heaving as we walked down,' Edwin said. 'A real buzz about the place. There's a fair few super yachts moored out in the bay too. I guess now the festival has kicked off the town will be even busier.'

After exchanging a quick look with Theo, when he gave her a

small shrug, Agnes said. 'Thank you for the offer to go to Monaco but I think Theo and I will have a quiet day here. I know Theo is waiting for a phone call and may have to go to Antibes Juan-les-Pins.'

Theo's phone buzzed at one point in the evening and Agnes held her breath as he stood up, murmuring, 'Excuse me, I need to answer this,' before he disappeared indoors. When he returned to the courtyard two or three minutes later he looked at Agnes and gave a slight shake of his head. Not Denice then as she'd hoped.

After Francine and Edwin left, Agnes and Theo had a nightcap of Saint Honorat liqueur out in the courtyard. 'I wish Denice would hurry up and return your call,' Agnes said. 'I worry that she's not going to ring you back.'

'I expect she's just busy and returning a phone call from a stranger isn't high on her list of priorities.'

'Maybe she associates the name Agistini with Oscar and doesn't want to contact you,' Agnes said.

'We have the address so we can always go and knock on the door until she opens it,' Theo said, smiling.

Agnes finished her drink and stood up. 'I think I'll have an early night. See you in the morning.'

Getting ready for bed, Agnes's glance was drawn to the envelope Theo had brought down from Oscar's. With all the excitement of knowing Denice was back in the Riviera she'd taken it upstairs with her and thrown it unopened onto the dressing table next to her *grandmère*'s newly polished table mirror that Theo had also brought down for her. Perhaps now would be a good time to open it? Of course, what she'd really like to do with it was to throw it away unopened but she wasn't brave enough to do that in case it did contain something of importance. Although what on earth Oscar could have to say to her after all these years she dreaded to think. Sighing, she reached out a hand to pick it up, when there was a knock on the door and Theo's voice called out.

'Denice has phoned.'

'Come in,' Agnes said, jumping up quickly, the envelope forgotten again. 'What did she say?'

'She apologised for the late call. Apparently, she's been away and only returned this evening. I've arranged to meet her tomorrow afternoon.'

'You didn't tell her about me?'

'No.' Theo shook his head. 'She was a little bristly at first, asked if I was related to Oscar Agistini. I told her he was my brother and that he had recently died. She asked me what I wanted to talk to her about. I told her it was a highly personal matter and I'd rather explain face to face. She then suggested three o'clock tomorrow afternoon and I agreed.'

Agnes sank down on her bed. 'I can't believe that tomorrow I'm going to meet up with my sister after all these years.'

36

Knowing that neither of them would be able to settle to doing anything before they left for the meeting with Denice, Theo suggested they drove to Juan-les-Pins and explored a little before having a leisurely lunch. 'There are several good restaurants there. Could even treat ourselves to lunch at the Hotel Belle Rives.'

'Not sure I'll be able to eat anything,' Agnes said. 'I feel so nervous but a wander around Juan would be good. Have you got the file?'

'Already in the car.'

Cannes was heaving with people and traffic was heavy as they left on the coast road and it took twice the time it usually did to reach the outskirts of the town where the traffic cleared a little.

Twenty minutes later, as they approached Golfe-Juan, Theo gave Agnes a quick glance. 'I think we have time for a quick detour.'

Agnes glanced at him, mystified, as he followed the sign for the Marina entrance car park, and pulled up in a space near the entrance.

'I phoned earlier and was told where Oscar's boat is moored. I think we should at least see it before it is sold.' He gave Agnes a questioning look as she got out of the car. 'Yes?'

She nodded. 'We haven't got all day though. I want to get to Antibes. How will we find it. I mean there are hundreds of boats here. Does it have a name?'

'The harbour master told me it is berthed alongside the main quay, which is here opposite, and about halfway down.' Theo led her along the walkway. 'We recognise it easily, I think,' he said. 'The name is on the stern.'

Agnes laughed. 'You need to tell me the name,' she said, walking quickly along. 'Goodness only knows what Oscar would call his boat – "*Mal Acquis*" maybe? It was certainly an ill-gotten gain.' Suddenly she stopped and stared at one of the larger boats before turning to look at Theo. '"*Agnes*"? Is this the one?'

Theo nodded.

'He took my money and then named the boat after me? *Quelle moquerie!*'

'But you will have the last laugh when the boat is sold,' Theo reminded her.

'Thanks to you. Let's go. I do not need to see any more.'

The two of them turned and made their way back to the car.

As they strapped themselves in, ready for the rest of the drive, Agnes leant across and kissed Theo on the cheek.

'What was that for?'

'Just because,' Agnes smiled at him. 'Where would I be without you?' Theo started the car and Agnes sat back in her seat, silently answering that question herself. Lost, that's where she would have been without Theo all these years, lost.

* * *

Half-an-hour later, as they drove past the 'Welcome to Antibes Juan-les-Pins' sign Agnes asked, 'Did Denice give you directions?'

'*Non*. I Googled it and I know where the street is,' Theo answered. 'But for now I think we find a car park and have a wander.'

The narrow streets were full of boutiques of all kinds and restaurants and coffee shops were everywhere. The restaurants on the beach with their wooden floors, sun canopies and ice buckets on every table to keep the wine cool were the busiest. With their kitchens on the other side of the road, Agnes lost count of the number of times she caught her breath as she watched the young waiters, typically carrying their trays on a raised arm across the road, dodging around the moving traffic.

'I never realised waiting could be such a dangerous job,' she said.

For their own lunch they decided on ham and cheese baguettes which they ate sitting on a bench overlooking the sea. Or rather Theo ate, Agnes couldn't swallow properly.

'Do you think she'll have changed much?' she said, turning to Theo.

'We all change as we grow older,' Theo said.

'I suppose what I really mean is – will she still feel like my big sister? Or will we be like complete strangers meeting for the first time?'

'I don't know,' Theo said, reaching for her hand. 'But you are still the same kind-hearted, truly decent person you've always been, despite what life has thrown at you. Hopefully Denice has survived her own life traumas intact as well.'

'I think we will walk to her house,' Theo said. 'According to the map it's not far from here. If we go through this little park just along here, I think we'll be heading in the right direction.'

Leaving the park, Agnes saw a florist further down the road and impulsively stopped to buy a bunch of flowers for Denice. It was too early in the year for Denice's favourite, sunflowers, so Agnes decided on a bunch of variegated yellow tulips.

They found Denice's house easily. One of a dozen in a small impasse, Number 5 was about halfway along. Tall Provençal green electric gates blocked the entrance. Agnes stood behind Theo as he pressed the intercom and gave his name. The small gate on the side clicked open and they stepped through into a large courtyard.

A short flight of shallow steps led up to the front entrance of a low, white painted villa. A woman was standing in front of the open door, leaning on a cane, watching as Theo walked towards her, Agnes was careful to stay behind him, out of sight as best she could.

'Monsieur, I did not realise you planned to bring another person with you. I wish you had mentioned it. I do not like surprises.'

'*Madame*, I'm hoping with all my heart that this is a surprise you will like,' Theo said, stepping to one side and leaving Agnes in full view.

'Hello, Denice,' Agnes said, her voice wobbling as she waited for her sister's response.

'Agnes? *Mon Dieu* is that really you? I never thought I'd see you again. Worse than that – I was afraid you were dead.' Denice flung her arms wide, her cane waving around precariously in the air. 'Come here. I need a hug from you.'

'Definitely still alive, and I definitely need a hug too,' Agnes said, quickly handing the flowers to Theo and moving towards her sister who looked in danger of falling over without the support of her stick. 'I thought you might be dead too. So, so, glad we're both alive.' The hug Denice enveloped her in was so tight she was soon struggling to breathe. Both Agnes and Denice's cheeks glistened with tears when they finally released each other.

Denice, turning to greet Theo, gave him a happy smile. 'Thank you,' she said, greeting him not with a hug but two cheek kisses.

'Let's go through to the garden. We'll collect a bottle of champagne on the way through. We need to celebrate while we catch up.'

'So much to tell you it's going to take days, weeks, to truly catch up,' Agnes said as she and Theo followed Denice through the house and out into the garden. A large swimming pool, its water glinting in the sunlight, was down at the far end. A paved terrace with palm and olive trees surrounded it, teak transats covered with comfy cushions had been placed around one side of the pool. Nearer the house was another terrace with wrought-iron garden furniture and a large parasol and it was here that Denice put the champagne and urged them to sit down.

'Theo, could you do the honours please,' and Denice passed him the champagne to open and pour. Once they all had a glass in their hands, Denice proposed the toast. 'To us. So happy to be in touch again. Tell me, how did you know I was here?' she asked.

'I found your name and address in a file when I was going through my brother's things,' Theo said. 'It was in the papers dealing with your parents' house and the inheritance they left both of you. I trust you received yours?'

'Yes,' Denice nodded. 'Why?'

'Oscar swindled Agnes out of hers,' Theo stated baldly. 'Forged her signature, kept people away from her, told lies about her health.' He shrugged.

'*Cet homme était un véritable bâtard,*' Denice swore under her breath. 'He always promised to pass on messages for me.' Denice turned to Agnes. 'I'm guessing you never received them.'

Agnes shook her head. 'Not one.'

'I came to Cannes once after our parents died,' Denice said. 'I found your house but Oscar wouldn't let me in. Told me you weren't well enough for visitors and I was to go away. I did knock on a few neighbours' doors but they were all incomers and nobody really knew Oscar. Kept himself to himself they said. There was one older woman two or three doors away who said she remembered a woman and a small child living there but she hadn't seen them for years.'

'Francine, my daughter, and I moved to the UK when she was seven,' Agnes said quietly. 'There's a lot to tell you but first I want to know all about what it was like living in Paris and if you became an actor like you dreamt of being. For years I kept looking out for your name whenever I saw a celebrity magazine.'

Denice sighed. 'Paris itself was wonderful. Not a lot to tell about the acting. Papa was right. I wasn't good enough. Took me a couple of years to give up on my dream though and boy were those tough years. Took time living on the streets to bring me to my senses and get my act together.' Denice paused and gave a rueful smile. 'Made some good friends at that time who helped me get a job and create a new life for myself. I did toy with the idea of coming home but Papa made it very clear the one time I called him that I was no longer his daughter.'

'I thought I saw you at the film festival one year,' Agnes said. 'I ran after you but you and the man you were with drove off in an official limousine. I decided it wasn't you in the end.'

There was a short silence. 'You did see me that day,' Denice said slowly. 'I did wonder if you'd recognised me. I was pleased to see the three of you looking so happy together. I consoled myself for years that at least you were happily married with a family.'

'Theo was with me that day, not Oscar, and I wasn't happily married,' Agnes snapped. 'So, why didn't you speak to me then?'

Denice bit her bottom lip and looked Agnes straight in the eye. 'Because I could not. I was working. It would not have been professional of me.'

'Working?'

'I did various things to survive and to make money.' Denice paused. 'One of my main sources of income for several years was working as an escort for an up-market escort agency before I started my own escort business. The day you saw me I was with a top Hollywood producer as his partner for his visit to the festival.'

Agnes sat back and looked at her sister in horror. 'Are you saying you became a prost—'

'*Non*,' Denice interrupted sharply. 'I was never a prostitute. A reputable escort agency provides legitimate escorts, both male and female, for people who need a companion for an event, or a hostess for a business function. There are lots of reasons people hire an escort. For me it was all about surviving the best way I could. Of course there are other less reputable agencies around but I never worked for them and mine was totally respectable.' Denice drained her glass. 'Enough about me. Your turn – you said you were unhappily married.'

Agnes, still reeling from her sister's matter-of-fact attitude to surviving when things were desperate said. 'Yes, very unhappily. I think we'll leave those details for another time. How about you. Did you ever marry? Do I have any nieces or nephews? And why are you using a cane?'

'Hip replacement a few weeks ago. To answer your other questions – no children. Married just the once.' Denice gave her a thoughtful glance. 'If you don't have to rush back to Cannes, can you stay for dinner?'

'Oh, I don't know,' Agnes said. 'What about Cerise?' she asked, turning to Theo.

'I asked Zazz to walk her when she got back from dress shopping,' Theo said. 'I can ring and ask her to feed her later.'

'Please do that,' Denice said. 'I'd like to introduce you to someone special to me.'

37

Zazz was beginning to despair of ever finding a dress that she liked enough to shell out the large number of euros they all seemed to cost. She and Mel had walked the length of rue d'Antibes both ways looking for her 'festival' dress. A couple of times she'd thought she'd found it until she looked at the price tag.

They'd stopped for a reviving coffee and cake when Mel pointed at a shop window on the opposite side of the road. 'Did we look in there? I don't remember seeing that green dress in any window.'

'I don't remember either,' Zazz said. 'Come on, let's check it out.'

'It's a second-hand shop,' Mel said with disappointment as they got closer. 'It might call itself Posh Vintage but it's second-hand stuff.'

'I don't have a problem with that,' Zazz said. 'Some vintage clothes are good quality and lovely,' and she pushed the shop door open.

The green chiffon dress in the window that had caught their eye still looked good close up. The assistant was happy to take it out of the window for Zazz to try on and showed her into the small changing room.

Strapless with a fitted bodice, the chiffon material of the simple design draped beautifully, a silk waistband of the same green emphasising the empire line sat perfectly positioned under Zazz's bust. Zazz pulled the curtain back. 'What d'you think?'

'Wow. Dominic won't be able to keep his eyes off you – and probably his hands,' she added, laughing at the look on Zazz's face. 'Does it feel good?'

Zazz nodded before turning to the assistant and asking the price. 'Originally it retailed for one thousand four hundred euros but now it is five hundred euros.'

'I'll take it. Could I try that white faux fur bolero on with it please?' Zazz said. 'I'm going to need something to keep me warm after the film.' The white bolero felt cosy and complimented the dress.

'It is an outfit that you will wear time and time again,' the assistant said as Zazz held her iPhone over the card machine to pay.

'Let's hope so,' Zazz said. 'Come on, let's find somewhere for lunch.'

Ten minutes later, sitting at a pavement cafe sipping glasses of wine, rosé for Zazz and white for Mel, whilst they waited for their salade Niçoise, Zazz glanced at her friend.

'Can I ask you about Dominic's last relationship? All he's said to me is that she wasn't an important part of his life.'

'Tara? She left him for the son of an Australian millionaire she met in Monaco. Dom wasn't heartbroken or anything, I think he'd realised she wasn't for him by the time she left.' Mel took a sip of her wine. 'What it did do though, was to bring back memories of Maman going off with the yacht captain and the way it affected Papa and us. Dom basically decided that he didn't need to open up himself to that kind of rejection. That was, of course, until you turned up.'

The waitress arrived with their *salades* at that moment and Mel fell silent until she'd moved away.

'He's definitely decided that you are special and worth taking the risk so don't you dare run off with anyone else, okay?' Mel gave Zazz a ferocious look.

'After that look I wouldn't dare,' Zazz said. 'I think he's special too,' she added quietly.

Mel had to leave to pick up some clients from the airport after lunch so Zazz made her way home and then down to Theo's to walk Cerise.

When Theo rang later that afternoon she happily agreed to walk Cerise again and to feed her.

'What time do you expect to be back from – where did you say you were?'

'I didn't but we're in Juan-les-Pins seeing as you asked and we've – we've met up with an old friend who wants us to stay for dinner.'

'Okay, I'll keep Cerise with me until about nine o'clock and then I'll pop her back to your cottage. Enjoy your dinner with your friend. Oh, tell Gran I've found the perfect dress to wear for the film festival.'

38

The someone special Denice wanted them to meet turned out to be her husband, Carl. Younger than her by more than a decade, he clearly adored her and she him.

Agnes was intrigued to learn how they'd met, they were such an unusual couple. Denice with her flamboyant sense of style and Carl a much quieter personality in every way. They'd met when Denice had been in her fifties and running her own successful escort business. Carl, an accountant, had needed someone to accompany him to a business dinner at The Ritz in Paris.

'I walked into her office, told her the kind of woman I would like to escort for the evening and asked her if she had anyone suitable available,' Carl said. 'And she told me she was fully booked. Turned out to be an outright lie.'

'It wasn't a complete lie,' Denice protested. 'That was a particularly busy evening. All my escorts, apart from one, were already booked. A couple were actually going to be at the same dinner. The one who was still available wouldn't, I knew instinctively, be right for Carl. That same instinct told me I was the perfect partner for him – and not just for the evening. We've been together ever since.' Denice took a sip of her wine. 'Tell me about Francine. To think I have a niece. Is she with you on this trip? I can't wait to meet her.'

'You also have a great-niece,' Agnes said. 'Francine has a daughter, Jasmine, known to everyone but me as Zazz.'

Sitting outside on the terrace in the warm night air, listening to the cicadas chirping away, enjoying the food and champagne Denice had provided, Agnes could see her sister was still very much the same person she'd known growing up. Whatever life had thrown at her, she'd been strong enough to retain a sense of her own self-worth.

Inevitably talk turned to the past. Childhood memories were dug up, shared, dissected and put away again with a different slant on them. It was a slightly tipsy Denice who stood up at the end of the evening as Agnes and Theo prepared to leave and put her arms around Agnes and gave her a serious look.

'I'm sorry that our parents took my departure from their life so seriously that they took it out on you by completely controlling your life. Forcing you to marry that evil man,' Denice shook her head. 'If it helps, I did, and still do, feel guilty for leaving you to cope with them alone. Please forgive me.'

'I forgive you but it wasn't all your fault. It was my fault too for not being brave like you. I should have stood up to them. I didn't. Luckily, I had Theo in my life. Without him I think Oscar would have destroyed me completely, if not killed me.'

'I'm so sorry,' Denice said.

Agnes gave her a smile. 'Let's look to the present and the future, forget the past as much as we can. We're back in each other's lives now. We need to fix a date for you to meet the rest of the family. Francine, Jasmine, and Edwin, Francine's husband. I'll give you a ring soon, okay?'

'Make sure you do. And we need a sisterly chat about you and

Theo. You are so perfect together. I can't understand why you didn't divorce Oscar and marry Theo years ago.'

'It's a long story,' Agnes said. 'One day I'll tell you all of it.'

* * *

Agnes was quiet on the drive home, lost in thoughts about Denice and the way her life had turned out. It seemed that it had been a question of surviving in a somewhat hostile world for both of them. The two of them had faced unexpected difficulties that they could never have imagined growing up. Denice leaving home in the way she did had created her own problems but she'd also left Agnes to carry the burden of problems instigated by her absence. Their father's determination to make Agnes obey him and live her life the way he deemed to be suitable had taken Agnes's freedom away. Her life had changed irrevocably because of her sister's somewhat selfish behaviour. But it was impossible to hold a grudge against her sister. She had done the only thing open to her at the time. Agnes could only wish that she'd possessed half of Denice's courage – and had defied her father by refusing to marry Oscar Agistini.

Denice's words about her and Theo being the perfect couple as they were leaving sprang into her mind. Dear Theo. He'd always been there for her. More of a husband to her than Oscar had ever been, protecting her, taking care of her and loving her down through the years despite being unable to be with her. He had been the one who finally enabled her to leave Oscar for a different, safer, life far away from his violence. The memory of that event totally engulfed her as she sat silently in the passenger seat while Theo drove them back to Cannes…

Francine had been at school one September morning and Agnes was at home alone when Theo arrived back from a tour. He'd been gone three months this time, leaving shortly after the film festival incident where she thought she'd seen Denice. Those three months had been hard. Pleasing Oscar had been difficult. Everything she did was wrong and she'd felt his fist more than a few times although he was usually careful to hit her in places she could cover up. Until the last incident three days ago when he'd pushed her so hard she'd lost her balance and fallen down the stairs, bruising her face on the banister and breaking her right arm as she landed in a heap at the bottom of the stairs.

Oscar had leapt into solicitous husband mode, driving her to hospital, explaining how she'd tripped on the rug at the top of their stairs to the nurses and doctors, and generally being seen to be a caring husband. Despite the pain in her arm, Agnes was secretly delighted when the lovely African nurse sternly told him to leave and go and wait in the relatives' waiting room. The last time Agnes had come in with bruises having 'walked into the kitchen door', that particular nurse had told her in no uncertain terms to leave the bully, that there was help available. But she had nowhere to go, so she'd stayed.

Theo, when he'd walked in that morning, had taken one look at the technicolour bruise on her face, the plaster cast on her right arm and had demanded the truth. Agnes told him. 'He pushed me down the stairs.'

'Where's Oscar right now?'

'Monaco for a business meeting.'

'Let's get you out of here then. Can you pack a few essentials for you and Francine? If you can't pack much don't worry, we'll buy whatever you need. When you've done that, we'll go and collect Francine from school. You are leaving here today. I can't bear to see you in this state.'

Agnes nodded mutely. She knew it was time. She couldn't take any more. And it was not good for Francine to grow up in such a toxic environment. She had no idea what Theo was planning but she trusted him implicitly. She'd do whatever he told her to do.

Thirty-six hours later, after the first flight for both her and Francine had passed in a blur, they'd landed in the UK. Theo had then driven them down to the West Country, telling Agnes that he was taking her somewhere he knew she'd be safe and away from Oscar. The final part of the journey had been on the Higher Ferry crossing the river to Dartmouth. Agnes, standing on the deck of the ferry, had looked at the small riverside town nestling near the mouth of the River Dart and had felt an easing of the tension that had settled in her body over the last few days. Somehow she knew that she would heal in this place. That she and Francine would be safe here.

For the next few days they'd stayed at a small B & B on the main road, whilst Theo sorted out a permanent place to rent, finally deciding on a furnished cottage in one of the lanes around the town. When Agnes protested she had no money to pay him back with, he hugged her and told her not to worry for now. Things would come right in the end and they'd discuss it then. She promised him that she would pay him back every penny as soon as she could. Theo went to the school to help her register Francine. He also introduced her to the English wife of an old musician friend of his who had settled in Dartmouth when his own band had disbanded. If she ever needed help with anything, Sylvie Aubert was the first person she was to go to, Theo said.

Both she and Francine were bereft when after ten days Theo had to leave them but he assured them he'd be back for Christmas. And he was – and for every following Christmas...

Theo noticed her wet cheeks when they arrived back in Cannes but didn't say anything until they were indoors when he took her in his arms and held her tightly. 'Was today too difficult? You must be happy that you and Denice have started to build bridges back together,' he asked, studying her face.

Agnes gave him a weak smile. 'It was a little difficult but so lovely seeing Denice again. Hearing her talk about how she survived stirred up my own memories of you rescuing me and taking us to Dartmouth, I owe you so much. I doubt I would ever have escaped from Oscar without your help. I know I've paid back the money you lent me down through the years but I can never repay you for your love, care and kindness to both Francine and me.'

'You've been in my life for over fifty years,' Theo said quietly. 'And that's the very least of what I dreamed of and always wanted – the love of my life, in my life even if it was difficult at times,' and he pulled her closer before bending his head and kissing her. As she kissed him back Agnes felt the happiness rising inside her.

39

There was a message from Suzette, the notaire's property manager, on the house phone when they reached home that evening asking if she could come and take photos and measurements the next day and suggesting an open morning some time before the festival finished. 'It is short notice but we already have clients on our books who have expressly asked us to look out for this type of property for them and who are currently in town. Once the details are on the website I am confident there will be a big surge of international interest, particularly from the Americans.'

Agnes rang the property manager early the next morning, agreeing to her suggestions. Francine, when she called her, immediately started to make plans.

'We'll need to style the house. Make it look as attractive as possible. We haven't got time to do any decorating so we'll just clean the place up as best we can. The day of the open house we'll put flowers in every room, coffee in the kitchen, no clutter anywhere. At least Zazz did the courtyard the other day. And we've already cleaned the bedroom that Oscar had let go. We'll make the bed up in there too.'

Agnes laughed. 'I don't think we need go overboard. The notaire clearly thinks whoever buys it will want to renovate and modernise, knock walls down and do other things.'

'I think we still need it to look as good as we can make it,' Francine said.

'Fine, but please don't expect me to come and help style it,' Agnes said. 'I'll leave that to you. Theo and I will cook you dinner tonight. See you around eight o'clock. You can tell us all about your visit to Monaco and there's something I need to talk to you about too.'

'Talk to me now,' Francine said.

'No, it will keep until then. Is Jasmine home at the moment?'

'Yes, but I know she's going out soon.'

'I'll ring her and tell her we'd like her to come for dinner tonight as well. I hope she is free.'

'Maman, what is going on?'

'I just need to talk to you and tell you something exciting,' and Agnes ended the call.

Agnes and Theo followed Theo's usual morning routine, which Agnes had readily adopted as her own – breakfast and then an early-morning visit to the market, followed by coffee at their favourite cafe. Once home, they prepared the ingredients for dinner that evening together. Agnes glanced at Theo and gave him a small smile as they moved around each other in the kitchen instinctively, they knew each other so well. She knew deep down that Denice had been right when she'd said that they made a perfect couple. If only they had been allowed to be that couple in the past.

* * *

Up at Oscar's, Francine and Edwin spent the morning 'tarting up the place' as Edwin called it. Zazz, out for the morning interviewing an English woman who was the chairperson of a Franco-British Society, promised to pick up some flowers from the market on the way home.

Edwin's phone pinged with an incoming message as they sat down to a well-earned cup of coffee and a pain au raisin after they'd finished. 'Ah,' he said as he read it, before glancing up at Francine.

'The e-mail you were waiting for?' she said.

'Yes, but still no definite date for the meeting I need to have. So a few days' reprieve before I have to return home.'

'I'm glad you don't have to rush back,' Francine said as the front door slammed. 'It's nice being down here together.'

'Is she here yet?' Zazz asked as she rushed in, clutching bunches of white roses and thrusting them in Francine's direction. 'I need to tidy my room before she gets here.'

'Dad and I made your bed,' Francine said as she filled two vases with water. 'And we threw shoes and things into the cupboard out of sight, so it's fine.'

'Thanks.'

As Francine divided the roses between the two vases, there was a knock on the door.

'I'll put these in the sitting room while you answer the door,' Zazz said.

Over the next hour and a half, Suzette measured every room, took lots of photographs and spoke lots of notes into her phone. After taking one final photograph of the courtyard she switched off her phone and turned to Francine and Edwin.

'Right. All done. I'll get back to the office and start the marketing. First time on the market in over fifty years, this house has got so much potential. I think, rather than put a definite price on it we'll ask for offers in excess of two and a half million euros and it will be snapped up quickly. I know similar houses further along the rue have been turned into two apartments and one apartment sold just last week for a million euros.'

Closing the front door behind Suzette, Francine went back into the kitchen in a daze. 'I can't believe that figure she's going to ask for offers in excess of, can you? So much money.'

* * *

Francine, Edwin and Zazz walked down together for dinner with Theo and Agnes that evening. After telling them about the estate agent's visit and the decision to ask for offers on the house, Francine turned to Agnes.

'So what is it you want to talk about, Maman?' she asked.

'A couple of things,' Agnes said. 'First, I need to tell you about the discovery of one of Oscar's more dubious dealings. Theo and I took some papers he had found going through the files to the notaire to check for us.' She took a deep breath. 'Oscar cheated me of my inheritance from my parents by lying about me and forging my signature. It would appear it was that money he used to buy his boat. A boat he called "*Agnes*".'

'Oh Maman, he really was wickedly immoral in the way he treated you,' Francine said.

'But I will receive the money when the boat is sold,' Agnes said with a smile. 'Thanks to Theo.'

'Let's go through to the courtyard. Theo has aperitifs waiting out there.' Agnes said. 'I have some really exciting news for you. And we want to hear about your visit to Monaco as well.'

'Zazz said you went to Antibes Juan-les-Pins to see an old friend yesterday,' Francine said, accepting an aperitif from Theo.

'We did,' Theo said, looking at Zazz. 'Thank you for looking after Cerise for me.'

'Anytime,' Zazz said.

'Do I know this old friend?' Francine said.

'No, but you know of her and you will meet her soon,' Agnes said. 'And I expect I will see a lot of her in the future.'

Francine looked at her puzzled. 'You will?'

'Yes. Your aunt Denice is looking forward to meeting you and her great-niece, Jasmine.' Agnes smiled happily as she waited for Francine's reaction.

'Your sister, Denice? The one that ran away?' Francine frowned as she looked her mother.

'Isn't it wonderful news?' Agnes said excitedly.

'Cool,' Zazz said. 'First Serge shows up, a half-brother for Mum and an uncle for me as well as Cousin Al who is a great-nephew for Theo. And now we've got a long-lost aunt and her husband. We're turning into quite the extended dysfunctional family.'

'Now she and her husband are both retired, they travel a lot. But she rang this morning to say she'd re-arranged things and she and Carl are coming over the day after the open house viewing to meet everyone.'

'Are you sure it's her? Not someone pretending to be your long-lost sister,' Francine said.

'Francine! When did you get so cynical?' Agnes demanded. 'Of course it's her. I know my own sister even if we haven't been in touch for years. And I'm so, so happy to have her back in my life. The least you can do is be happy for me. *Donc*! Let's change the subject, *maintenant*. Tell us about your day in Monaco.'

'It was a good day,' Edwin answered, realising that Francine was upset by her maman's outburst. 'Wouldn't want to live there though. So busy and touristy. We saw some beautiful boats and the visit to the Casino was amazing.'

As they all tucked into their duck confit, with pan-fried potatoes and a green *salade*, talk turned to the marketing of Oscar's house.

'The house is as ready as it ever will be, except for the finishing touches on the open day,' Francine said, regaining her equilibrium. 'I just hope the notaire and Suzette are right when they talk about it selling quickly. You don't think maybe they are over pricing it?' she said glancing at Theo.

'*Non*,' Theo said. 'Property up there is much sought after. They know that they have a property that is going to earn them their commission quickly.'

'Not too quickly, remember I'll be homeless when it sells,' Zazz said. 'It's a few months until September when I move in with Mel.'

'You could take it as a sign,' Francine said. 'A sign that you should give up this silly idea of yours and come home and find another job.' She registered the disapproving look Edwin gave her and smothered a sigh. It was so difficult to step back, not to sound critical whenever she made a suggestion and she knew Zazz would have taken those words as interference on her part.

'Sorry, not my business,' Francine mumbled, picking up her glass of red wine and taking a sip.

'Not going to happen, Mum,' Zazz said. 'Mel has already said I can sleep on her sofa bed.'

'And there is always a room here for you,' Theo said quietly. 'So you don't have to worry about her having nowhere to live,' he added, turning to Francine.

'Thanks, Theo,' Zazz said gratefully. 'Anytime you need Cerise looking after, I'm your girl.'

40

The morning of the open house viewing organised by the notaire's office dawned bright and sunny. Francine was up early to give everything in the house a final polish and to put fresh flowers in the sitting room. Suzette would be there from about 9.30 and there was a steady stream of viewers booked in every ten minutes from 9.45 onwards. The notaire had stressed that the people viewing were all serious buyers and said it was best if they left the agent to show everyone around. Once Suzette arrived, Francine and Edwin left her to it.

'What's Zazz doing this morning?' Edwin said.

'She said she was going to spend the morning doing some research in one of the museums,' Francine said. 'And then she's got a hair appointment at mid-day ready for this evening.'

'So do we have any idea what we are going to do this morning?' Edwin asked.

Francine shook her head. 'Pretend we're on holiday and mooch around? We need to think about how much longer we're going to be here too. Not that I'm desperate to leave but we can't stay down here forever.'

'We could if you wanted to,' Edwin said.

Francine looked at him in surprise. 'Are you serious? Our lives are back in Devon and Maman lives there.'

'Maybe Agnes will decide to move back here now that Oscar is dead.'

'That's a possibility, I suppose,' Francine said. 'Especially now that Denice is back in her life.'

'I think Theo will have a bigger influence on her than her sister. The two of them seem to have grown closer than ever in the last week or so,' Edwin said.

Francine was silent for a moment. 'Do you honestly think after all these years that's likely to happen?'

Edwin nodded. 'I do, but only time will tell if I'm right. So shall we spend the morning window shopping in various estate agencies?' he said. 'Just for fun. Pretend we are going to come and live down here?'

'It will be something to do this morning,' Francine said, laughing. 'So long as we don't get carried away with the idea. Because I honestly don't think it's feasible. First though, I vote we have a coffee in Piers's cafe.'

A couple of hours later, when they returned to Oscar's, they found Suzette sitting in the kitchen typing rapidly on her laptop.

'Hi. Just waiting for the final couple to finish their second look and then I'll get out of your way. Back to the office and await developments.' She smiled at them. 'From some of the comments, I'd guess we will receive some serious offers soon.'

* * *

Zazz carefully took the green dress off its hanger and slipped it over her head at the same moment there was a gentle knock on her bedroom door.

'Can I come in?' Francine called out, a hesitant note in her voice.

'Please. You've timed it perfectly – you can zip me up.' Zazz turned her back towards her mother gratefully. She was sure there had been a bit of a sea change in her mother's attitude towards her recently for some unknown reason. Less bossy and abrasive, more like she had been before the house move to Dartmouth.

'Are you looking forward to this evening?' Francine asked as she gently slid the zip up.

'Yes, but I'm also feeling a little nervous,' Zazz confessed. 'Do I look okay? I'm not used to physically being in the limelight, I'm usually showcasing something or someone else on social media. Not showing off myself in public. Having said that, could you take a photo of me? I probably need one for Insta if nowhere else.'

'The dress is lovely and you look beautiful in it,' Francine said. 'The colour really suits you. Where's your phone?'

Zazz pointed to it on the bed. 'Over there.'

After Francine had taken the photo, Zazz glanced at her. 'I'm very grateful you arrived in the nick of time to zip me up, but did you come up for a reason?'

Francine smiled at her and gave a small shrug. 'I just wanted to see if you needed a hand getting ready and to say...' She hesitated. 'I'm sorry if I've been difficult lately. I'd not exactly forgotten you are all grown-up and independent these days, but I've found it hard trying to manage the difference between inadvertently interfering or simply giving you some motherly advice that you can choose to take or to ignore.' She paused. 'And of course on top of everything else it didn't help that you came down here without a word to anyone, to meet Oscar.' She held up her hand as Zazz went to speak. 'It's fine. I understand why you did it. I just feel sad that I made it too difficult for you to confide in me about how you felt. Anyway, Dad's downstairs waiting to see you all glammed up, so I'll leave you to finish your makeup. And I'll see you down there.' Francine closed the bedroom door behind her as she left.

Five minutes later, Zazz went downstairs to join her parents in the sitting room and to wait for Dominic. When he arrived he was happy to enjoy a small aperitif with her parents before they left hand in hand for the Palais des Festivals.

41

With only three more nights to go, the film festival might be drawing to the end but still the hype continued to build excitement around which film would win the coveted Palm d'Or on Sunday evening, and which actors would personally win awards as people tried to second guess the panel's decisions before Sunday evening.

Zazz stood at the beginning of the red carpet clutching Dominic's hand as they waited their turn to begin making their way along the carpet and up the steps into the Palais des Festivals. 'I can't believe I'm here,' she whispered. The paparazzi, four or five deep in places, were everywhere, shouting at celebrities walking up the famous twenty-four steps to 'give us a smile' or 'look this way'.

'Believe it.' Dominic squeezed her hand. 'You'll be blinded by flashlights as soon as we start to walk. You're looking so lovely tonight everybody will be wondering who you are.'

'Thank you, but look who is in front of us,' Zazz said. 'Isn't that the teenager currently at the top of the charts with her hit song? Nobody will notice me after her. Which will be quite a relief. I can't imagine living life in the public eye like she and all the other stars do.'

'Here we go,' Dominic said. 'Shoulders back and smile. It's our turn to walk the walk.' Zazz took a deep breath and strolled as confidently as she could at Dominic's side on to the red carpet where the two of them were greeted by a salvo of flashlights going off from all directions.

'Told you,' Dominic muttered. Zazz gulped and tried to smile. What was it everyone was supposed to want? Fifteen minutes of fame? Maybe this was hers.

Once they were seated in the packed auditorium Zazz breathed a sigh of relief. 'Well, that should make your day,' Dominic whispered. 'Look at who's sitting over there. George and Amal.'

'I can now claim to have been in the same room as them,' Zazz giggled. As the lights dimmed Dominic's hand claimed hers and they settled back in their seats to watch the film.

Two hours later, as the lights came on, Zazz wriggled in her seat and looked at Dominic. 'Please don't ask me if I enjoyed that.' She sighed. 'If only George had been in it.'

'Come on, let's follow the crowd and get out of here,' Dominic said, laughing. 'I think we both deserve a drink after sitting through that.'

By the time they were descending the red carpet, the crowds were smaller but the paparazzi were still hanging around, waiting for the last of the celebrities to appear. Nobody took any notice of Dominic and Zazz though as they stepped off the red carpet onto the pavement and disappeared into the streets of Cannes out of the limelight.

'Are you pizza hungry?' Dominic asked.

'That sounds like a good idea,' Zazz said. 'Will anywhere be open at this time of night?'

'Festival week they open all hours. Come on, my favourite is this way,' and Dominic held her hand as they crossed the road and began to walk towards the Allées de la Liberté where Zazz could see the restaurants were still open and busy.

Sitting there sipping glasses of red wine while they waited for their pizzas, Zazz looked around her. 'This place is truly something else during film week, isn't it? It's lively and buzzy at other times but for the ten days of the festival it seems to take on an extra vibrancy, almost a magical air about it. Dreamlike and romantic, it feels surreal to me. I love it.'

'Monday morning, it will be back to reality,' Dominic assured her. 'There are other very busy festivals and conferences throughout the year, but they do lack the glamour of this one. I like to travel to see other places, but I love coming home and honestly, I wouldn't want to live anywhere else,' Dominic said.

Their pizzas arrived at that moment and they both tucked in and it was a moment or two before Dominic said. 'Mel is thrilled you're going to share her apartment from September.'

'Not half as thrilled as I am,' Zazz said. 'It's such a lovely place.'

'So, you're planning on living down here for the next six months? Or longer?'

'If everything goes to plan – and please don't tell my mother this – I'm not planning on going back to live in the UK any time soon. I love it down here. Of course it does depend on me really upping my followers on Instagram and YouTube by several thousand to survive. I've got a bit of a cushion but you never know what the future is going to bring.'

'My future is suddenly looking a lot brighter hearing that you are staying,' Dominic said. 'We can really get to know each other, if you want to.'

Zazz smiled at him. 'I'd like that a lot.'

42

Friday morning and Agnes could barely contain her excitement at the thought of Denice and Carl coming for lunch to meet Francine and Jasmine for the first time. When Theo returned from giving Cerise her first walk of the day, they went to the market as usual but today they were buying ingredients for a special lunch. The weather forecast promised a hot day with the temperature possibly hitting twenty-seven, so they decided rather than cook they'd provide a cold lunch. Lots of cheeses, a board of charcuterie meats, some langoustines, a big green *salade* and several artisan breads from their favourite boulangerie. Dessert would be a big bowl of fresh local strawberries with crème fraîche. And champagne of course. It was a special occasion.

Back at Theo's, as they sat out in the courtyard enjoying a palmier biscuit with their coffee, Agnes glanced at Theo. 'Has Francine said anything to you about wondering if Denice is really my sister?'

'*Non*. Why?'

'She was so suspicious that day we told her about meeting

Denice, I thought she might have questioned you about how you felt about her.'

Theo shook his head. 'I think you were so definite about Denice being Denice that she took your word for it finally.'

'I hope so. I don't want any awkward conversations spoiling today,' Agnes said.

Theo smiled at her. 'Stop worrying. Everything will be fine. Come on, time to start getting the place ready. What time did you suggest to everyone?'

'Around mid-day.'

Francine and Edwin were the first to arrive. Agnes felt her heart sink as she sensed how uptight Francine was about this meeting with her unknown aunt. Before she could say anything to reassure her, Denice and Carl arrived in the flurry of exuberance that Agnes seemed to remember her sister always generated around her when socialising, making it impossible to ignore her. Calling her the life and soul of any party she attended had been the only way to describe the teenage Denice.

Once indoors, Denice turned to Francine and pulled her into a tight hug. 'You have no idea how much this means to me, first re-uniting with Agnes and now meeting my unknown niece. That bastard, Oscar, has a lot to answer for. Thank God he's dead, we're all better off with him out of the way. Anybody ever told you how like your maman you are?' Francine nodded her head, hardly able to breathe the hug was so tight.

Releasing her, Denice turned and took Edwin's hand in a firm grip before planting two kisses on his cheeks. 'And you must be the husband. Lovely to meet you.'

The front door slammed at that moment and Zazz flew into the room. 'Granny, I'm so sorry I'm late. I hope Great-Aunt Denice hasn't, oh, you have,' and Zazz came to a quick halt as she saw everyone. 'Hello, I'm Zazz.'

Denice, her arms outstretched, advanced towards her. 'If you call me great-aunt ever again I shall disown you. I'm Denice, understood?'

Zazz nodded. 'Understood.'

'In that case, come here and let me hug you.' As Denice threw arms around Zazz she whispered in her ear, 'And I promise I'll never call you Jasmine.'

There was a carefully controlled pop as Theo eased the cork out of the champagne bottle before pouring everyone a glass. 'Time for a toast,' he said as Zazz handed the glasses around. 'To family.'

'Family,' they all echoed.

'You all right, Mum?' Zazz asked quietly as Denice followed Agnes into the kitchen. 'You look a bit dazed.'

Francine smiled. 'I don't think our lives are ever going to be the same again with Denice in them.'

Edwin's phone pinged at that moment and with an apologetic look at everyone he excused himself and went outside to answer it.

When he returned five minutes later he whispered to Francine, 'I have to leave tomorrow.'

'Will you come back down? Or shall I leave tomorrow with you?' she asked quietly.

'I should only be away for two days at the most and I was planning on coming back down to spend more time here with you.'

'I'll stay and wait for you to come back then,' Francine said. 'Then we can go home together in maybe a week or ten days.'

* * *

Zazz, up early to go for her now routine daily run with Mel, said goodbye to her dad before leaving. He was waiting for the taxi to take him to the airport for his morning flight back to the UK, having declined Theo's offer to take him so early in the morning.

Mel was waiting for her in their usual meeting place and soon they were running along the quay. 'So how was the long-lost aunt yesterday?' Mel asked.

'She's great. *Flamboyant extrovert* best describes her, I think,' Zazz said. 'Would you believe she ran an escort agency for years? You'd never lose her in a crowd. Complete opposite of Granny but you can see they're sisters. She was really interested in my social media stuff. Said she was going to look me up, follow me and tell all her Parisian friends about me and this is the exciting bit.'

Mel glanced at her.

'She has a contact with the Press Office at the Palais des Festivals and she's going to try and get me a general pass as a "Content Provider", which, I didn't realise, is another form of publicity the Press Office uses these days for all the events at the Palais, not just the film festival. I've promised to love her forever if she can pull that off.'

'Talking of love, my brother is wandering around with a silly look on his face,' Mel said. 'Very similar to the one that appears on your face when his name comes into the conversation.'

Zazz laughed. 'I've told you – we're just friends, for now,' she added. 'Right, time to turn round and buy the breakfast croissants. Got to keep Mum company for breakfast as Dad's gone back home for a couple of days.' It was too soon to admit to Mel, or anyone, exactly how she felt about Dominic.

43

Late Saturday afternoon, Agnes and Theo were preparing to go for a walk to soak up the atmosphere of the penultimate day of the festival when Monsieur Caumont rang.

'I have received a very good offer for the house from a cash buyer and I would advise you to accept it,' he said. 'The buyer would like completion within weeks rather than months, which I don't think is a problem for you? The time scale is more a problem for me than you.'

Agnes thanked him, accepted the offer and said the early completion date was not a problem for them. In fact, they'd welcome a quick completion date.

As they left for their walk Agnes and Theo talked about how quickly the house had sold. 'And for such a high price. I know Monsieur Caumont said it was a desirable property but it's a lot of money.'

'Property down here is expensive,' Theo said. 'And the fact that the house hasn't been on the market for years does make it desirable in people's eyes.'

'It's such a relief to know that soon it will be someone else's and out of my life for ever,' Agnes said.

'Will you stay down here while it all goes through?' Theo asked quietly. 'Or return to Devon and come back here for the final signing on completion day?'

'I think I'll—' Agnes stopped. 'I don't know. It sounds as though the sale might go through quicker than usual so it might be better to stay. But at the end of the day my life is over there and I will have to return at some point.' She shook her head.

'You're happy down here, aren't you?' Theo said quietly.

'Yes, I am.'

'Then please stay. Change your life to over here.'

'I don't think it's that easy a decision to make,' Agnes said. 'There's Francine and Edwin to consider as well as Jasmine.'

'Jasmine is already living over here,' Theo pointed out. 'And probably intends to stay for as long as possible, Let's go home. I need to do something.'

'Oh, okay,' Agnes said, surprised at the abrupt end of the conversation and the walk they'd hardly begun.

Theo was silent on the way back to the cottage and once indoors he made for the sitting room.

'Please sit down. I want to play you something.'

'I've been longing to ask you to play the piano since I arrived,' Agnes said. 'I do wish you hadn't given up on the saxophone.'

Theo regarded her intently for several seconds before moving across to the piano, pulling out the stool, gently, thoughtfully, stroking the keys before he started to play the one tune guaranteed to reduce Agnes to an emotional wreck.

She closed her eyes as the lyrics of 'Windmills of Your Mind' began to swim through her mind. So many words resonated with her. She knew she had always loved him and yet had done nothing but hurt him in the most awful way. She fingered the

Celtic pendant that she rarely took off these days and tried to hold the tears at bay.

As the last note died away Theo swivelled on the piano stool, turning to look at her and saying her name in such a way that made her look at him anxiously.

'I think the memories that song triggers mean everything to both of us,' he said, his eyes fixed on her necklace. 'I love seeing you wear that necklace,' he said quietly. 'You never wore it on my visits to see you and Francine in Devon. I did not think you still had it.'

'I treasured it down through the years. I often just held it, hoping to feel close to you.'

'And did you?'

'I found the trick was to hold the necklace and play our song but then I couldn't stop crying. I didn't wear it for years. It was too poignant a reminder of what I'd lost through my own stupidity. These days, I rarely take it off.'

'I do so love having you here, please stay,' Theo said. 'You complete my home – and my life.'

Agnes shook her head. 'We agreed a long time ago not to talk about what might have been.'

'*Je sais*, I know. But I cannot help but think, hope, pray, that now things are different our friendship will finally be allowed to flourish into the relationship we've both wanted for so long? And still want.' He gave her a hopeful look. 'Maybe now is the time to follow your heart. Which is something I've always urged you to do.'

Agnes hesitated. 'You don't think it is too late for us?'

'You are finally free of a marriage that caused you so much heartache and pain and are free to move forward. It's never too late when you love someone,' Theo said. 'We can be together like we've dreamt of for years. It's never too late to be happy and in love.'

Agnes smiled. 'It would be rather wonderful, I have to admit. But you forget, you live in France and I live in England.'

'Pff, when everything is sorted it will not be a problem. I come to you. You come to me. We decide. We can be together wherever we choose. Six months here, six months there. We can work it out if you are willing to try?'

There was a short pause before Agnes spoke. 'If you want me to,' and she gave him a tremulous smile.

'Agnes, I don't want you to leave me ever again. I've dreamt of living a life somewhere with you ever since I met you. Now finally the two of us have the opportunity to have a proper relationship. Why d'you think I've never married? You are the only woman I've ever wanted to marry.'

Agnes pressed her lips together in an effort to stop herself crying at his words. 'But you could have had a family of your own. I'm so sorry I was the reason you didn't.'

'You, Francine and Zazz are my family, always have been, always will be,' Theo said. 'Nothing will ever change that, I promise you. I know I repeat myself *mais* I so love having you here,' he said. 'When everything is settled, I hope you will decide to stay with me – we can sort out the logistics of where – but we will finally be together – as we've always wanted to be and deserve to be.'

* * *

Saturday evening and Francine was at a loose end, feeling unsettled and missing Edwin although he hadn't been gone twenty-four hours yet. She was alone in the house, Zazz having gone out earlier to spend the evening with Dominic. Briefly, she wondered what Agnes and Theo were up to, before deciding they'd probably appreciate a few quiet hours after the excitement of the last day or two.

Bored and flipping through one of the glossy boating magazines of Oscar's that they'd left on the shelf, Piers came into her thoughts. Would he be down on his boat this evening? He had said he was there most evenings but maybe Saturday night was different. Saturday evening was the time for socialising with other people, for parties. Impulsively, she decided to go and buy a takeaway pizza and see if Piers would like to share it with her. If he wasn't there she'd come back and eat it here, alone.

Half an hour later, clutching both a pizza and a bag of frites, Francine was anxiously approaching Piers's boat. Her heart missed a beat when saw him in the cockpit, alone.

'Fancy some company? I've got supper if you're hungry,' she called out.

'This is a good surprise,' Piers said, helping her on board. 'You didn't have to bring food but I'm suddenly longing for a slice of pizza.'

Five minutes later, Piers had opened a bottle of wine and they were tucking into their food.

'Where is your husband tonight?'

'He's had to return to the UK for two days,' Francine said. 'Zazz is out with a certain Dominic,' she raised her eyebrow quizzically at Piers who simply smiled at her. 'Which is why I've had to bribe you with food to keep me company and to stop me feeling alone like Billy No-Mates.'

Piers looked at her, puzzled.

'Strange English expression,' Francine said.

'You don't have to bribe me with food to keep you company,' Piers said quietly. 'I like your company but I suspect Edwin is a little wary of our friendship.'

'I've already told him how close we were in the past but now we're older and just good friends with a long friendship history.'

'Good friends with history,' Piers repeated slowly, looking at her.

'Yes,' Francine said firmly. 'We'll keep in touch now we've connected again.' She hesitated. 'We'll always have a special friendship.'

'*D'accord*, a special friendship,' Piers said slowly. 'More wine?'

Francine held her glass out. 'Thanks. Oscar's house has sold,' she said, realising they were treading on dangerous ground and wanting to change the subject. 'So that's one problem being sorted. You know I told you about the possibility of this Serge Cortez being my half-brother? Well, it turns out that he is. I have met him, I took your advice and relaxed and when we met, we got on. He was surprise number one in my life. Having to share the inheritance with him is a bit of a blow, particularly for Maman, but it is what it is. At least Maman is finally getting some money from Oscar.'

Piers nodded thoughtfully. 'That's good. Surprise number two is? Please don't tell me you have more half-brothers, or even sisters, arriving in your life?' Piers said.

'No. Surprise number two was Maman's long-lost sister, Denice, turning up.' And she quickly explained how that had come about. 'I'm just waiting for surprise number three now,' she said, laughing. 'Everything always comes in threes, doesn't it?'

'*Peut-être* surprise number three will be my Dominic and your Zazz getting together,' Piers said.

'Aren't they together already?' Francine said before realising what he meant. 'Rings being exchanged you mean? Making it official.'

Piers nodded. 'It would be ironic, wouldn't it?'

'It would be rather nice,' Francine said. 'But if it happens, it won't happen soon. Zazz is determined to make a success of being a "social media influencer".' She pushed away the unbidden, unexpected thought of what might have happened between herself and Piers years ago. It was far too late for those 'what-if' kind of thoughts.

The town hall clock could be heard striking the hour and with a start Francine realised it was eleven o'clock. 'I'd better get back to the house. Otherwise there is a good possibility my daughter will lock me out.'

'I'll walk you back,' Piers said, standing up. 'No argument,' he said as she went to protest. 'It's late.'

Walking back, Francine was glad of Piers at her side. Saturday night revellers were out in force and she knew she could have attracted the wrong sort of attention if she'd been alone.

At the house door, Piers gave her a rueful smile. 'It's a long time since you and I were here saying goodnight.' He gave her a gentle kiss on both cheeks. '*Bonne nuit, mon amie spéciale.*' And he was gone.

Glancing up the stairs as she went in, Francine saw the light from Zazz's room shining down the spiral staircase. Impulsively she called out. 'Fancy a hot chocolate nightcap?'

'Please. Give me five minutes and I'll be down.'

'Stay where you are. I'll bring it up when it's ready,' Francine said.

When she carried the two mugs of hot chocolate up to the attic room, Zazz was just closing down her laptop.

'I thought you were out with Dominic this evening?' Francine said, as she handed Zazz her drink.

'I got back about an hour ago and decided to do some content preparation for next week,' Zazz said. 'You, on the other hand, were out late?'

'Pizza and frites with Piers on his boat,' Francine said. 'I was feeling a bit low and needed some company. You were out, I didn't want to interrupt Maman and Theo, so…' She shrugged. 'Piers is an old friend. We've still got lots of catching up to do.'

'Mum, you know I'm moving in with Mel in September?'

Francine nodded as she drank her drink.

'This place has sold so quickly that even if I wanted to stay here on my own, which I don't honestly fancy doing, it would only be a week or two before I'd have to get out. Granny added her voice to Theo's in insisting it made more sense for me to live down there for the rest of summer, so, when you and Dad go back home I'm going to move in with Theo for a few months.'

'Good idea,' Francine said. 'Granny will come home with us, I expect, so Theo will be glad of your company. And I'll be happier knowing he's keeping…' Her voice trailed away as Zazz gave her a look and shook her head. 'Sorry. Habit. I know you don't need anyone keeping an eye on you.'

Finishing her drink, Francine stood up. 'I'm ready for bed. See you in the morning, sleep well.'

Down in her bedroom, Francine hummed happily to herself as she got ready for bed. She and Edwin were rekindling their close relationship, and she and Zazz seemed to be understanding each other better. And having Piers back in her life as a friend, that was good too. The icing on the cake would be her inheritance. Deciding what to spend it on would be fun. Maybe they would buy a small apartment down here as a bolt hole. Life was definitely good at the moment and when Edwin returned it would be even better.

44

———

Later in her room, after saying goodnight to Theo, Agnes thought about what he'd said and smiled to herself. The idea of them finally living together as a couple had always seemed to be a distant, unobtainable, dream to her but Theo seemed adamant it was now within their reach if they wanted it. And she did want it very much.

The still unopened envelope on the dressing table caught her eye and she picked it up. Absently she ran her finger under the seal. A final hateful message from Oscar? Or an apology from him for his treatment of her down the years? If she was a betting woman she'd put money on it not being the latter one. But a hateful message could simply be thrown away and forgotten. Should she do that? Leave it unopened and burn it? *Non*. She simply couldn't do that.

As she took a folded piece of paper out of the envelope another piece of paper came out with it and fluttered to the ground. Without looking at it, she picked it up and placed it with the envelope on the dressing table. She opened the folded piece of paper and saw Oscar's familiar handwriting and began to read the last letter to her from her dead husband.

To my wife, Agnes Agistini,

It is thanks to Zazz, my so called 'granddaughter', that I am able to write this letter. A strand of her hair was SO useful.

Cast your mind back to the week before our marriage – a marriage I know you longed to be free of from the beginning, which was why I never divorced you. That particular week I went for a long weekend in Monaco with my friends. My brother, although invited, refused to join us.

I had often wondered about Francine being a honeymoon baby, as everyone assumed.

Zazz arriving unexpectedly in my life provided me with the opportunity to discover the truth. The DNA results are enclosed.

Jasmine Mansell is not, not, I repeat, my granddaughter.

Which raises the question whose granddaughter is she, and more importantly – who was Francine's father? Mon Dieu, that would be my brother, Theo, wouldn't it? I always knew he was in love with you. Part of the reason I married you was to stop him having you.

Recently I have learnt that I have a son – something you were unable to give me. Under French law, as my illegitimate son, he will be entitled to my estate – you will get what the law stipulates the remaining spouse receives and Francine will get nothing.

I have enclosed the DNA results for you to see and give to the notaire, he will know how to proceed even though they were not done via the French court.

Oscar.

Trembling, Agnes reached out and took the piece of paper from the dressing table. After studying it for several moments, she replaced both it and Oscar's letter in the envelope before sinking down onto the bed.

That special night in Antibes with Theo on the boat came into her mind. She'd never for one moment even dreamt that Francine had been conceived that night. She'd never given a thought that she might fall pregnant. All she'd known that night was that she loved Theo and wanted him.

How was he going to receive the news? She knew he adored Francine, had loved being in her life as her uncle but how would he react to learning that for the past fifty-three years he could have been so much more.

There was only one way to find out. First thing in the morning, she'd show him the letter and the evidence that Francine was his daughter, not Oscar's. She could only pray that he would welcome the unexpected news.

45

After a disturbed night, Agnes was awake before the sun rose the next morning. Knowing there was no chance of getting any more sleep, she dressed quickly and went down to the kitchen, taking the envelope and its contents with her. She popped a pod into the coffee machine and stood silently watching as the coffee came through.

Five minutes later, when Theo appeared, she took one look at him and burst into tears. He was immediately at her side. 'What's the matter? Are you ill?'

Agnes shook her head. 'No, I'm not ill. I don't know what I'm feeling right now,' she sniffed. 'It's a good job that Oscar is already dead because at this moment I could murder him with my bare hands.'

'What's happened?'

'Remember that envelope with my name on it? I finally opened it last night.' She picked up the envelope and took out the letter. 'He wrote me this letter and also gave me proof of what he says in it.'

'May I read it?' Theo asked quietly.

'Oh definitely, you need to,' Agnes nodded and handed it to him. The two minutes it took Theo to read the letter and glance at the DNA results, were two of the most worrying minutes Agnes had ever experienced as she waited for his reaction. Finally, he looked at her.

'I'm so sorry,' Agnes whispered.

'I have just one question I have to ask. Did you know all along that I was Francine's father and kept the knowledge from me?'

'No, of course not. That evening in Antibes when we made love I never gave a thought to becoming pregnant.' Agnes shook her head violently. 'Oscar, when we were on honeymoon, kept talking about the babies we would make and I believed, like everyone said, that Francine was a honeymoon baby. If I'd known she was yours I'd have told you. It could have changed everything. I wouldn't have kept it from you.'

'I didn't think you would. You and I have always been totally honest with each other. I do wish I'd known about Francine being mine earlier but I am grateful to know now. We'll have to take this to Monsieur Caumont so he can legally do what is necessary.' Theo put the letter down on the table.

Agnes gave a weak smile. 'Not sure what he's going to make of this new development.'

'I don't care what he makes of it,' Theo said. 'I couldn't be happier with the news. I meant what I said the other day – you and Francine have always been my family and now it's official.'

'We also have to tell Francine and Jasmine,' Agnes said. 'I think Francine will be happy with the news. As for Jasmine, I think your elevation from great-uncle to grandfather will no doubt delight her.'

* * *

Monday morning, and Agnes and Theo made their way to Monsieur Caumont's office. With no rendez-vous, they told the receptionist that they needed to see the notaire urgently as something had come to light that would alter the way Oscar's will was dealt with dramatically. Within five minutes they were shown into his office.

'Thank you for seeing us,' Agnes said as she held out the envelope. 'Clearing out Oscar's papers, in addition to the folder you already know about, Theo found this envelope with my name on it. I finally opened it last night. You need to see the contents.'

Carefully, the notaire took the envelope's contents out and read them. He looked up at Agnes quizzically as he shook his head. 'The estate of Monsieur Oscar Agistini continues to throw up yet another surprise. So now, after you receive your legal quarter share of the estate, the remaining three quarters will be inherited by Monsieur Serge Cortez alone. I will notify him of the change to his position now that he is the only child of Oscar Agistini. I think he will be pleased about it. Have you informed Madam Francine Mansell about her changed circumstances yet?'

Agnes shook her head. '*Non*, we plan on doing that later today.'

'*Bon*. Do we think this, irregularity shall we call it, with the deceased's will, is the last?'

'I sincerely hope so,' Agnes said.

As the notaire showed them out he turned to Theo with a smile. 'May I offer you belated congratulations on the safe arrival of your daughter.'

Theo laughed. 'They are certainly belated but appreciated all the same.'

* * *

Agnes was quiet as she and Theo walked back from the notaire's. 'I wonder how Francine will react to losing her inheritance from Oscar,' she said.

'I don't think she will be too upset,' Theo said pensively. 'She didn't have a lot of time for Oscar and has always said she didn't want anything from him. Her main concern has always been that you should get something, so I think on the whole, she'll be quite philosophical about it.'

'Hope so,' Agnes said. 'When are we going to tell them?'

'As soon as possible. Zazz too. We could walk up to the house now if you like, see if they are there.'

'Let's do that – and make it my very last visit to the house,' Agnes said.

Zazz stepped out of the house just as they reached it. 'Gran. Theo. What are you two doing here? I thought you were never going to darken the door of this house again,' she said, laughing.

'This is the last time,' Agnes said. 'We need to talk to your maman and you. Are you in a hurry or can you stay for a little while?'

Zazz glanced at her watch. 'I can hang around for about ten minutes, need to get to the library to do some research before it closes for lunch,' and she followed them into the house. 'Hope you haven't come to tell us about another lost relative. I'm telling you Mum will freak out if you have.'

'Not exactly,' Agnes said quietly. Zazz looked at her, surprised, but didn't say anything. 'Mum is in the kitchen.'

'Maman, why are you here?' Francine jumped up as Agnes walked into the kitchen.

'I promise you it's the last time ever,' Agnes said. 'Any chance of a coffee?'

'I'll do the coffees,' Zazz said.

'Agnes and I have just come from the notaire's,' Theo said.

'Oh, what now?' Francine sighed. 'Please don't tell me our buyer is dropping out.'

'No, it's not that,' Agnes said, taking a deep breath. 'First, I need to take you back to before you were born. I was in love with Theo and he with me and we had one glorious day and evening together as a farewell before I did as my parents insisted and married Oscar.' She turned to looked at Francine. 'You remember the envelope you found with my name on it in Oscar's bureau? I finally opened it last night. It was a letter from Oscar but it also contained the results of a DNA test using a strand of Jasmine's hair.' Agnes stopped speaking and took a deep breath. Before she could continue, Theo took hold of her hand and began to speak.

'The test showed that Zazz was not his granddaughter,' Theo said. 'Which made him wonder who your father was. He knew how close Agnes and I had been before the wedding so of course he had no difficulty in putting two and two together and realising the clear answer is me. I am your father and Zazz's grandfather. And I have to say, although it is a huge shock, I couldn't be happier.'

A stunned silence greeted his words.

'Well, I think it's great news,' Zazz said, placing the coffees on the table and breaking the silence. 'Cos, you've always been in our lives and you're just the perfect grandfather I've always dreamt of having. No longer Uncle Theo but Grandad.'

Francine reached for a coffee as she sat down. 'Did you really have no idea?'

'*Non*, I'm still coming to terms with the news,' Agnes said. 'But, like Theo, I couldn't be happier. The fact that Oscar is not a blood relation to you and Zazz but that Theo is...' She smiled. 'It's wonderful news.'

'I can't quite believe this,' Francine said. 'Have you two been having an affair for over fifty years?'

'Sadly no,' Theo said, smiling. 'But we have been special friends. I have loved your mother for all of that time. You are the result of the one night, before Agnes married Oscar, that we have spent together. And like everyone else we assumed that you were a honeymoon baby.'

'The other thing it changes,' Agnes said, speaking into the silence that had fallen. 'I'm afraid you are now no longer in the will. You will receive nothing.'

'I wanted to give it to you anyway,' Francine said. 'To make up for,' she shrugged, 'you know, the past.'

Agnes smiled. 'I wouldn't have taken it but thank you. I'm sorry you won't get anything directly from Oscar but I promise I will make sure you will receive something in the future.'

'You will still get something though, won't you?' Francine said.

'The small legal share that a wife gets when her husband dies.' Agnes nodded. 'French inheritance is strange like that, unless the wife is specifically mentioned, everything goes to the children. There is no special provision made for a spouse other than the right to live in the house until death, or if the house is sold, one quarter of the estate, the remaining three quarters goes to the children. In this case Serge Cortez.'

'I'm so sorry that not knowing the truth has caused so many problems down the years,' Agnes said. 'And it's all my fault for marrying the wrong brother. I've always loved Theo. I wish I had been allowed to marry him all those years ago.'

Theo squeezed her hand. 'We will be together now for the rest of our days. Perhaps even married?' He asked as he leant in and gave her a kiss.

* * *

After Agnes and Theo had left and Zazz had gone to the library, Francine realised she was trembling with the shock of the bombshell that her maman and Theo had just dropped. She picked up her phone, praying that Edwin would be free and able to answer. Relief flooded through her body as she heard his voice.

She stumbled over her words, almost choking as she got them out. 'You're not going to believe this,' she took a deep breath. 'Oscar left Maman a letter – with an illegal DNA test he had done in England. He used a strand of Zazz's hair, of all things.' Francine bit her bottom lip as she paused to try and calm down. 'It seems you were right. Maman and Theo are a lot closer than I've ever realised. Oscar isn't, wasn't, my father. But it turns out that Theo is.'

There was a two or three second silence before Edwin spoke. 'Well, that's unexpected news but good on the whole, I think? You've always hated Oscar but you've always loved Theo. And better to have him as a blood relative than Oscar?'

'Oscar clearly jumped at the chance to take advantage of Zazz's unexpected appearance,' Francine said. 'I knew Zazz sneaking down here to see Oscar would end in tears with him taking advantage of her presence.'

'But surely they're tears of happiness now,' Edwin protested. 'You should be grateful to her. It was her arrival in Oscar's life that enabled the truth to come tumbling out. You've gained a man you know and love as a father. I know you've lost an inheritance, but I don't think you really wanted anything from Oscar, did you?'

Francine shook her head. 'No. I simply wanted to make sure Maman finally got some money out of him.'

'I think Agnes has got everything she ever wanted now,' Edwin said.

'I'm glad it has finally worked out for them to be together,' Francine said. 'They've both suffered through Oscar's actions.'

She paused. 'I suppose I should think about coming home. I miss you and there is no need for me to stay now. Maman doesn't really need me now, besides she's got Theo ready to help her if she needs help.'

'I was going to surprise you tomorrow,' Edwin said. 'I'm booked on a morning flight. I should be with you at about two o'clock.'

'Oh, brilliant news. Shall I ask Theo to meet you?'

'No, I don't want to bother him. I'll get the tram into Nice and then pick up a train. See you tomorrow. Love you, Frankie.'

'Love you too,' Francine said smiling at the nickname as she ended the call.

46

The news the next day that the buyers had signed and paid the notaire all the agreed monies, including an extra sum for a very early completion date, was received with relief by everyone. Agnes though, was by far the happiest. Soon her life would be totally free of Oscar and his immoral ways that had somehow managed to weave a tangled web around her life for so long and kept her sister away from her. Agnes and Denice spoke to each other every day now and Agnes was loving having her sister back in her life. Denice was a real breath of fresh air and never held back from expressing her feelings about Oscar, 'the evil bastard', to quote her words.

Agnes knew Theo was counting down the days to when his brother's all-entangling threads in their lives would finally be cut and they could move forward together. She also realised that when Francine and Edwin returned to their everyday life in the UK, they were expecting her to go with them. At least Francine was. Edwin, Agnes suspected, was more in tune with the way things were between her and Theo now that she was free.

She couldn't bear the thought of leaving him even for a week.

They were so close now. She knew that Theo wanted her to stay and was acting as if it were already decided she would with the plans he was making for them. Of course, she knew that at some stage she'd have to return to the UK to sort things out but she intended to put it off for as long as possible – and then she and Theo would go together.

In the meantime, she had to tell Francine and Edwin that she wasn't returning with them to Dartmouth. Assure them she knew her house was in safe hands with them until they all decided what to do with it.

* * *

When Edwin arrived home that afternoon, Francine flew into his arms and held him tightly. 'I'm so pleased you're back,' she said. 'How was Dartmouth?'

'Fine – not as warm as here but sunny,' Edwin said, releasing her. 'I missed you not being there. Fancy going for a walk? Getting some fresh air? Maybe a *glacé*?'

'Yes. I can talk to you as we walk. I can't seem to sort out how I feel about Oscar not being my father and Theo taking his place. You're the only person I can really talk to about it.'

By the time they were walking along the Croisette, hand in hand, she was explaining how muddled she felt. 'I have no difficulty in accepting that Maman and Theo are now most definitely a couple but it's thinking of them as my parents that I can't get my head around. Maman is obviously still Maman but Uncle Theo, although I haven't called him Uncle for years, simply Theo, is different. Him suddenly turning out to be my father doesn't mean that I can equally suddenly start calling him Papa, even though I love him and am happy that he is my papa. I'm truly glad to be his daughter.'

'Have you talked to him or Agnes about this?' Edwin asked.

Francine shook her head. 'No. I don't want to hurt him. He's so proud of me, Maman says he tells anyone who will listen about his newly discovered daughter.'

'I think you need to talk to him, or at least to your maman,' Edwin said. Francine nodded. 'I think you right. I'll talk to Maman first. Explain that it's going to take me time to call him Papa but I do love him and hope they both understand.'

'Zazz, of course, hasn't got any problem with calling him Grandad – she does it at every opportunity, which makes me feel even worse.'

'She's young and the young always seem to accept change easier than us older mortals,' Edwin said comfortingly. 'You wait, another few months and you'll be "papa-ing" all over the place.'

Francine laughed. 'I hope you are right.'

* * *

'Maman, Theo, a couple of things. Edwin and I are thinking we will go home either the afternoon of the day when the sale of Oscar's villa is completed or the day after. It will depend on flights. Are you happy with that? Or is it too short notice for you?'

The four of them were sat around the table in the courtyard at Theo's enjoying a pasta supper. As Francine asked her question, Agnes sensed Theo tense as he listened for her reply.

'*Non*, it is not short notice for me because I am not leaving. Now we are finally able to be a couple I am staying with Theo.'

'You're staying for the summer. That's okay,' Francine said. 'We can come down again when you are ready to return.'

'Theo and I will come to Dartmouth together, when we are ready,' Agnes said in a voice that brooked no argument.

Francine, finally realising what her maman was saying, looked from her to Theo and back. 'What about your house?'

'It is your home for as long as you want it to be,' Agnes said. 'Our arrangement doesn't need to change just because I might not live there permanently again.'

'Okay,' Francine said, slowly turning to Theo. 'The other thing is, we might need a bed for one night. We can always go to a hotel but—'

'There's always room here for you,' Theo said. 'You don't have to ask. This is also your home now. Why not move down in the next couple of days?'

'Thank you.' And Francine gave him a grateful smile.

Later, as they walked up to Le Suquet, Edwin said. 'Do you want to think about moving down here seriously now that your maman seems intent on staying down here. We did see some nice villas the other day.'

'I know but it is such a huge step – even if all my family turn out to be living down here. I think we need to go back home, give it some serious thought and then decide what we do.'

* * *

Packing their suitcases in readiness to move down to Theo's was quickly done, which turned out to be a good thing. Monsieur Caumont rang Agnes to tell her they would complete the following day. As soon as they knew, Edwin rang to book their flights and was lucky enough to get seats on an early evening flight for the same afternoon.

As she left the house for the last time, Francine surprised herself by feeling a little emotional and bit her lip. This time in Cannes had made some good memories and whilst she wouldn't remember this house with a great deal of affection, leaving it today did mark the end of an era in her life, finally giving her closure.

'Hi Maman,' Francine said when they arrived at Theo's. 'I've locked the house up securely – where shall I put the keys?'

'Give them to me and I'll put them on the hook in the kitchen where Theo keeps all his keys. I'll take them to the notaire when I go,' Agnes said, holding out her hand for them.

47

Completion morning and Agnes and Serge found themselves sitting next to each other at the notaire's. Monsieur Caumont and another notaire with power of attorney, acting for the absent buyer, went through pages and pages of legal jargon requiring initials on every page – either theirs or the new owners or both. It took over an hour to be completed and for the keys to be handed over to the other notaire and for monies to be transferred to bank accounts.

As they left the notaire's Agnes heaved a sigh of relief. 'That took a lot longer than I was expecting,' she said. 'Buying and selling a house in England is far less complicated at that final stage. All that initialising of paper, and the reading aloud of clause after clause.' She shook her head. 'Come on, let's get back to the cottage. We both deserve a drink.'

Theo had suggested a small celebration party after the notaire's visit would be good. As he was now officially Serge's uncle he decided it was his responsibility so he would host it at the cottage.

When Agnes and Serge walked in they found Theo, Edwin,

Francine, Zazz, Rachel and Al all waiting impatiently for their arrival. The champagne was in the ice bucket and plates of aperitifs were on the table.

'So who are the new owners?' Zazz asked as Theo handed round the champagne. 'Anyone famous?'

'No idea,' Serge answered. 'They weren't there. Their notaire had power of attorney and signed everything on their behalf.'

'As for their name, Monsieur Caumont had difficulty in pronouncing it and I can't even remember it,' Agnes said. 'I daresay we'll hear eventually but I'm not really interested, to be honest. I'm simply happy that the place is out of my life now, I have some money, Serge has his rightful inheritance and everybody can now move on.'

'Let's raise a toast to that,' Theo said. 'To new beginnings and our extended family.'

'New beginnings and our extended family,' they said as they all clinked glasses.

* * *

Two hours later and the Cortez family had left and Edwin was carrying his and Francine's suitcases downstairs ready for their departure. Theo had insisted he would drive them to the airport and the luggage was soon being loaded into the car.

Both Francine and Edwin hugged Agnes tight as they said their goodbyes.

'We'll see you again soon,' Francine said. 'You take care. Don't let Zazz take advantage.'

'As if I would,' Zazz protested as she hugged her mum.

'Our granddaughter can take advantage of us as much as she likes,' Theo said, helping Edwin put their suitcases in the car.

'That's what grandparents are for. And I, for one, will not complain.'

After watching them drive away, Agnes and Zazz returned indoors. Zazz going straight upstairs for something and a thoughtful Agnes going into the kitchen to make them both a coffee. She'd noticed recently that Zazz was quieter than usual and she guessed that something was bothering her which she was determined to get to the bottom of.

Upstairs in her new bedroom, Zazz picked up a box from the boulangerie she'd bought earlier and gave a happy sigh. She knew Mel's sofa bed wouldn't have been that comfy and September was a long way away. Besides, living here for the next few months gave her the opportunity to get to know Theo better in his new role as her grandad, something she was really looking forward to. But first there was something she needed to say to Agnes whilst they were on their own.

Back downstairs she handed Agnes the boulangerie box. 'I thought we might need cheering up a bit so I've bought a couple of strawberry tarts,' Zazz said, pulling out a kitchen chair and sitting down, Cerise instantly at her side.

'Gran, I know you and Grandad are really happy but I still feel guilty that I came down here sneakily like Mum says and everything fell apart because of a strand of my hair.'

Agnes gave her a thoughtful look. So that was what was bothering her. 'If we'd given the notaire the go-ahead for the paternal DNAs to be done it would have fallen apart in a few weeks anyway,' Agnes said. 'Honestly, Zazz, it is good the truth has come out. Please don't give it another moment's thought. I'm the happiest I've ever been and so is your grandad. We're both very grateful to that strand of your hair. Eat your tart.'

Zazz stared at it her. 'You just called me Zazz, not Jasmine.'

'You can thank your grandfather and Denice. They both told

me I should call you what you wanted to be called. I was apparently showing my age by insisting on using your proper name and not going with the modern nickname.'

Zazz got up and hugged her. 'Thank you.'

They'd finished their coffee and tarts when Zazz's mobile buzzed. Dominic.

'Excuse me, Gran.' Zazz said, standing up and going out into the courtyard.

Agnes watched her fondly. Dominic was a lovely lad and clearly very fond of Zazz. She had a good feeling about that relationship.

* * *

Zazz was out with Dominic, and Theo and Agnes were eating a late supper out in the courtyard under a full moon, later that day, when Theo said, 'There is one loose end we still have to tie up before we are completely free of Oscar.'

Agnes looked at him. 'Which is?'

'Oscar's ashes.'

Agnes sighed. 'I'd forgotten all about them. Are they still in the cupboard?'

Theo nodded. 'Yes.'

'Do we scatter him somewhere he'd hate as a bit of karma? Or somewhere he liked? On your parents' grave here in Cannes?'

'I was thinking you and I could take a moonlit walk tonight along the beach and sprinkle them in the Mediterranean. He liked the sea.'

Agnes was quiet. 'Okay. Let's do that.'

'There shouldn't be too many people about,' Theo said. 'And once it's done, we can move on with our lives.'

An hour later and knowing that Cerise was curled up on

Zazz's bed waiting for her new favourite person to come home, something she'd done every night since Zazz had moved in, Theo took the urn out of the cupboard, placed it carefully in a canvas shoulder bag and they quietly left the cottage.

There were still a few people about even though it was late. Hand in hand they walked towards the beach. A few of the restaurants on the bord de mer were still open and they quickly crossed the road and walked along the sand.

There were a few other couples walking along the shore and they made sure to avoid them. 'D'you think they are doing what we're planning to do?' Agnes whispered. 'If they are, Oscar will have plenty of company.'

'No, I think they're having a romantic walk along a moonlit beach,' Theo said.

They walked until they reached a completely deserted area of the beach when Theo carefully took the urn out of the bag and took the lid off. 'I'm going to carefully shake it as we walk,' he said. A few minutes later he said. 'There you go, Oscar. I can't say it was a pleasure being your brother but I wish you well in eternity.'

Agnes stayed silent. She had nothing left in her to say to Oscar, even in farewell.

Turning to walk back, Theo caught hold of Agnes's hand and turned her towards him.

'Now he's out of our lives forever, Agnes, my love, will you marry me?'

'Yes,' Agnes instantly replied. 'Whenever and wherever you like.'

Theo pulled her towards him and held her tight as they sealed their love and new-found happiness with a kiss.

EPILOGUE
ONE YEAR LATER

Denice and Carl are hosting the wedding reception for Agnes and Theo in the garden of their villa in Juan-les-Pins after their marriage at the Hôtel de Ville Antibes. Agnes hadn't wanted to marry Theo in the Mairie in Cannes and Antibes has been the perfect venue choice. Francine, in the English tradition, agreed to be matron of honour and Zazz was thrilled to be her gran's bridesmaid. Agnes can scarcely believe that she has finally married her true love. As for Theo, he knows he is the happiest and the luckiest man in the world to be able to call Agnes his wife. As they stand side by side to cut their single-tier wedding cake, Agnes finds herself reflecting on how much her life has changed since Theo phoned to tell her that Oscar was dead. A death that changed everything for ever in her world.

Denice can barely keep the tears at bay, she is so happy for her sister – and for herself. Being back in touch with Agnes has brought so much joy into her life. She adores Francine and treats Zazz like a favourite grandchild who can do no wrong. Denice and Carl are frequent visitors to Cannes and the two sisters are as close as they've ever been.

Francine and Edwin finally decided to move down to be closer to Agnes and Theo and Francine confessed she was missing Zazz. They have just bought a lovely villa in Mougins, a short drive from Cannes. Edwin has taken up golf and his handicap is improving the more he plays. Francine still works as an editor occasionally but decorating the new villa is taking up a lot of her time and she has got very involved with the local Sunny Bank Charity, especially the second-hand book side of it. Theo is delighted that his daughter now calls him Papa every time they meet.

Zazz has moved into the Belle Epoque villa with Mel and is ridiculously happy. Denice's contact in the Press Office at the Palais des Festivals was happy to register Zazz as a Content Provider for several of the conferences and exhibitions held in the Palais, including the film festival. She still writes a lifestyle column for Marcus, and now regularly sells features to the English national papers and several glossy magazines. Agnes is expecting to hear any day now that Dominic has placed a ring on her finger.

The Cortez's are part of their extended family these days and Rachel and Serge with his wife are here this afternoon. Al had a previous engagement and couldn't make it. Rachel is currently feeding Cerise tiny bits of ham from the wedding breakfast still laid out on the table.

As everyone eats their cake and drinks their champagne, Denice signals to the trio of musicians on the swimming pool terrace and they pick up their instruments. Agnes looks at Theo as the notes of 'Windmills of Your Mind' begin to drift on the air towards them. Theo holds out his hand and when she takes it, he pulls her towards him, takes her into his arms, and together they begin to sway gently to the melody that is definitely 'their tune'.

* * *

MORE FROM JENNIFER BOHNET

Another book from Jennifer Bohnet, *A French Country Escape*, is available to order now here:

https://mybook.to/CountryEscapeBackAd

ACKNOWLEDGEMENTS

Huge thanks go to the Boldwood Team as usual for being the brilliant publisher they are. Special thanks to my editing team Caroline (patience of a saint) Ridding, Rose the copy editor and Rachel the proofreader.

Thanks to all the bloggers out there doing such sterling work getting books noticed and big thanks to the admins and readers of two of my favourite book groups The Friendly Book Community and Riveting Reads and Vintage Vibes.

And finally, but by no means least, a huge thank you to all my readers.

Love, Jennie.

Xxx

ABOUT THE AUTHOR

Jennifer Bohnet is the bestselling author of over 14 women's fiction titles, including *Villa of Sun and Secrets* and *A Riviera Retreat*. She is originally from the West Country but now lives in the wilds of rural Brittany, France.

Sign up to Jennifer Bohnet's mailing list here for news, competitions and updates on future books.

Visit Jennifer's website: www.jenniferbohnet.com

Follow Jennifer on social media:

facebook.com/Jennifer-Bohnet-170217789709356

x.com/jenniewriter

instagram.com/jenniewriter

bookbub.com/authors/jennifer-bohnet

ALSO BY JENNIFER BOHNET

Villa of Sun and Secrets

A Riviera Retreat

Rendez-Vous in Cannes

A French Affair

One Summer in Monte Carlo

Summer at the Château

Falling for a French Dream

Villa of Second Chances

Christmas on the Riviera

Making Waves at River View Cottage

Summer on the French Riviera

High Tides and Summer Skies

A French Adventure

A French Country Escape

Secrets Beneath a Riviera Sky

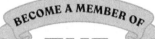

Boldwood

Boldwood Books is an award-winning fiction publishing company seeking out the best stories from around the world.

Find out more at www.boldwoodbooks.com

Join our reader community for brilliant books, competitions and offers!

Follow us
@BoldwoodBooks
@TheBoldBookClub

Sign up to our weekly deals newsletter

https://bit.ly/BoldwoodBNewsletter

Printed in Great Britain
by Amazon